DOC SAVAGE'S AMAZING CREW

William Harper Littlejohn, the bespectacled scientist who was the world's greatest living expert on geology and archaeology.

Colonel John Renwick, "Renny," his favorite sport was pounding his massive fists through heavy, paneled doors.

Lieutenant Colonel Andrew Blodgett Mayfair, "Monk," only a few inches over five feet tall, and yet over 260 pounds. His brutish exterior concealed the mind of a great scientist.

Major Thomas J. Roberts, "Long Tom," was the physical weakling of the crowd, but a genius at electricity.

Brigadier General Theodore Marley Brooks, slender and waspy, he was never without his ominous, black sword cane.

WITH THEIR LEADER, THEY WOULD GO
ANYWHERE, FIGHT ANYONE, DARE EVERYTHING—
SEEKING EXCITEMENT AND PERILOUS ADVENTURE!

THE MAN OF BRONZE
THE THOUSAND-HEADED MAN
METEOR MENACE
THE POLAR TREASURE
BRAND OF THE WEREWOLF
THE LOST OASIS
THE MONSTERS
THE LAND OF TERROR
THE MYSTIC MULLAH
THE PHANTOM CITY
FEAR CAY
QUEST OF QUI
LAND OF ALWAYS-NIGHT
THE FANTASTIC ISLAND
MURDER MELODY
THE SPOOK LEGION
THE RED SKULL
THE SARGASSO OGRE
PIRATE OF THE PACIFIC
THE SECRET IN THE SKY
COLD DEATH
THE CZAR OF FEAR
FORTRESS OF SOLITUDE
THE GREEN EAGLE
THE DEVIL'S PLAYGROUND
DEATH IN SILVER
THE MYSTERY UNDER THE SEA
THE DEADLY DWARF
THE OTHER WORLD
THE FLAMING FALCONS
THE ANNIHILIST
THE SQUEAKING GOBLINS
MAD EYES
THE TERROR IN THE NAVY
DUST OF DEATH
RESURRECTION DAY
HEX
RED SNOW
WORLD'S FAIR GOBLIN
THE DAGGER IN THE SKY
MERCHANTS OF DISASTER
THE GOLD OGRE
THE MAN WHO SHOOK THE EARTH
THE SEA MAGICIAN
THE MEN WHO SMILED NO MORE
THE MIDAS MAN
LAND OF LONG JUJU

LAND OF LONG JUJU

A DOC SAVAGE ADVENTURE
BY KENNETH ROBESON

A NATIONAL GENERAL COMPANY

LAND OF LONG JUJU
*A Bantam Book / published by arrangement with
The Condé Nast Publications Inc.*

PRINTING HISTORY
Originally published in DOC SAVAGE *Magazine January 1937*
Bantam edition published April 1970

Published simultaneously in the United States and Canada

*Bantam Books are published by Bantam Books, Inc., a National
General company. Its trade-mark, consisting of the words "Bantam
Books" and the portrayal of a bantam, is registered in the United
States Patent Office and in other countries. Marca Registrada.
Bantam Books, Inc., 666 Fifth Avenue, New York, N.Y. 10019.*

PRINTED IN THE UNITED STATES OF AMERICA

Chapter I

RUNNERS TO DEATH

Two weird figures came running in the white fog. Their queer garments flapped like the sheets of ghosts. Runners of the jungle should not have been so dressed. The togalike attire was pulled above bony knees, but the garments were hampering. Any white man who had been in Abyssinia would have identified these sheets as the *chamma*. This was distinctive of royal or official rank.

These grotesquely clad runners were far south of Abyssinia. They were now below the great Taveta forest of Central East Africa, in the foothills of the Parri Mountains. It was a green, fog-soaked wilderness of silence just now.

Doubtless the place was too silent in the judgment of the taller of the two runners. The pair was approaching a water hole.

The taller runner halted suddenly. He held up one long, skinny arm. The other runner became motionless. Both listened intently.

There came only a strange, distant throbbing; like the hard heel of a human hand beating upon some hollow vessel. The runners knew the sound for a drum. The stretched skin of a *kuda,* the great antelope of the country, over the end of a hollowed *senecio* log.

The runners had been hearing the drum talk for two days and two nights. Five days and nights before, when they had started, there had been six runners. Only these two had survived to reach this place.

"*Safi maji,*" whispered the tallest runner hoarsely.

He meant the pool contained clean water. Some other pools had been poisoned. Two of the original six runners had drunk of these pools.

These two had remained behind.

1

The taller runner directed his companion to drink while he kept watch. The skin drum continued to throb.

The shorter runner dropped to his hands and knees. He crept through the white fog to the pool. His brown hands divided the broad leaves of a *senecio* tree.

No sound had been given forth by the fog-drenched leaves. The taller runner rasped a warning. The shorter runner stretched on his stomach. His tongue lapped up water where his hand had pushed away the scum.

Then he made a sudden, violent effort as if to rise. His neck seemed incapable of lifting his head. His face splashed into the pool. Air bubbles arose around the man's head.

The tall runner made no effort to rescue his companion. He whispered a word.

"Okoyong." Then he added, "Masai, the Long Juju."

The tall runner seemed almost to dissolve into the wall of the jungle. His companion was already a stiffening body. A small dart had appeared behind one ear of the runner who had died beside the pool.

Though he had been running for five days and nights, halting only when overpowered by sleep, the tall man slipped through the tangled vines of the liana with amazing speed.

THE tall figure was the last of the six runners. On the shoulders of this single man rested the burden of the message that had been carried by six.

Whatever the encircling menace, the runner escaped temporarily. He carried but a single weapon. This was a sharp-bladed, short-hafted stabbing spear.

He had said, "Okoyong" and "Masai." No fiercer tribes dwelt in all of Africa. The Masai were blood-drinkers and head-hunters of this interior central country. The Okoyong were from a distant place. They had come into the land of Kilimanjaro, bringing witchcraft, the worship of the Long Juju.

Perhaps the tall runner had no hope of escaping with his life. But his message must be delivered verbally.

More than one drum was talking now. The taut skins throbbed from four points of the compass.

The runner's face was different from that of other tribes in the Kilimanjaro and Taveta forest country. His skin was lighter than the smoky black mostly to be found. The nose was thin and hawklike, an arching bone that might have belonged to an ancient Roman rather than to a native of Africa.

The thin nostrils now were twitching. The runner's keen olfactory sense told him he was not far from his goal. The odor was that of meat being cooked as only an *Inglesi* would want it. All white men were *Inglesi*, or Englishmen.

The runner came to a wide, open glade beside a flowing stream of white water. His thirst was very great, almost unendurable.

The man hesitated for less than five seconds. His long legs plunged him forward into the open space. Then he cried out, only once. The impeding *chamma* fell down around his knees and entangled his legs. The stabbing spear flew from his hand.

The man lay still, except for a twitching of his muscles. From his back, between the shoulder blades, protruded a long spear haft. Ostrich feathers, dyed red with ochre, quivered in the wind.

"It was in this direction I heard it," spoke a deep, resonant voice in English with a broad American accent.

A white man pushed aside the vines. He started into the open space where the sheeted figure lay with a spear in his back.

A big native, wearing only a garment of colobus monkey fur, thrust an ebony arm in front of the white man.

"No like, *b'wana!*" he grunted. "Me first go see!"

But the white man was bigger. He pushed past the restraining arm. He looked like a giant beside the other. His figure was huge, an immense bulk of perhaps more than two hundred and fifty pounds.

"Thunderation, Souho!" he boomed. "That fellow's still living! Maybe we can save him! Here, grab a hatful of water!"

The huge white man swept off his helmetlike, tropical hat and thrust it into the native's hands.

"Hurry, Souho!" he commanded. "We'll see what we can do!"

"Will make do, *B'wana* Renwick," muttered the native.

Souho obeyed the order of *B'wana* Renwick. He reached the stream by keeping close to the jungle wall.

"Come, give me a hand, Mapanda," said *B'wana* Renwick.

"I've got a hunch that fellow was trying to get to our *safari*. Maybe he's from old King Udu himself."

A quick-moving youth with a yellowish skin and snapping black eyes moved behind the white man. Mapanda was of an Arabian cast, probably from one of the upper coastal tribes.

B'wana Renwick had faced too many dangers in too many outlandish places to betray any fear.

For the white man was Colonel John Renwick, world famous engineer. To thousands he was known simply as "Renny." He was one of the world's most noted group of adventurers.

Clark Savage, Jr., known to the world as Doc Savage, was soon to know of this dead native runner in the African jungle. For, as Renny lifted the head of the dying native in the strange *chamma*, Doc Savage, in New York, was attempting to get in touch with the giant engineer over the world's most powerful short-wave radio.

WHEN Souho, the native hunter, brought the hat filled with water, the dying runner gulped some of it. Renny lifted the man in his arms. Death was certain. The blade of the spear had pierced the man's body.

"*B'wana—B'wana* Renwick?" whispered the dying man. "It is good you come—Ras Udu—the king of Koko is going —"

The runner's head dropped. Renny quickly produced a small hypodermic syringe. In a few seconds, the man opened his eyes. Whispered speech came to his lips through bloody foam.

Renny held him in his arms. The words were partly English and partly a native patois.

"Yes?" he said, when the runner halted and choked. "King Udu wants the railroad? And what is this other?"

The runner could say only a few words. His speech ended. Renny pulled the *chamma* over the man's face.

"Doc's got to know about this," he said slowly to himself. "Come, Souho! Mapanda! We'll take the body to camp! He must be buried!"

Souho and Mapanda, Renny's head carrier, did not relish this task. Souho, the hunter, was a brave man. He had faced a man-eating *simba*, the great lion of the Taveta, with only his spear. But he carried the body of the dead runner as if it were some dangerous high explosive.

Equatorial night descended upon Renny's camp as they arrived with the body. Already the carrier boys had a great fire going.

The skin drums had never ceased talking. The throbbing was spaced between beats like dots and dashes of the regular Morse telegraph code.

The carriers were eating. Their meal was a delicacy with them. It consisted of elephant feet baked for two days in a hot pit.

"Hyrax no make much talk, *B'wana* Renwick," said Souho. "The spear is of Masai, *b'wana*. It means they make do war."

"Holy cow!" growled Renny. "And if they make do war, as you call it, they'll bust up the whole railroad scheme! Them Britishers won't back any steel into war country right now!"

The night was oppressive. There had been no visit of the small colobus monkeys. Renny had been on this railroad survey for nearly six weeks. The small monkeys had followed the camp.

Only an engineer of outstanding ability could have plotted the line of steel from Muoa Pemba, on the Indian Ocean south of Mobasi, through the Parri Mountains to the great Taveta country. The line was intended to open up the rich lands of the Kilimanjaro mountains.

Renny believed their camp was being closely watched. The silence of the hyrax and the absence of the monkeys in the dense jungle could mean only one thing. Many men must be close to the camp.

RENNY brought from his tent a huge square box. From this he produced a radio transmitter. The transmitter was one of Doc Savage's system. Its short wave made it possible for his men to reach him across many hundreds of miles.

Renny set the dials to the wave lengths employed by the Doc Savage group. Mapanda's black eyes glittered. To this native's mind, *B'wana* Renwick was a greater sorcerer than the most powerful Juju priests.

The generator started humming. Still the drums were talking.

Suddenly one of the carriers let out a wild screech. Others of the native boys threw aside their platters of elephant feet.

The screech became a death scream. A native boy arose.

His bony body teetered back to its heels. He fell in the edge of the big fire. His flesh burned sickeningly.

The blade of a long spear stuck through the carrier's throat. Before Renny could get to his feet, two more native boys were impaled. The other carriers howled and dashed toward the denser jungle.

"Come back, you fools!" roared Renny. "Make cover here!"

Renny was whispering into his tent. Screams of agony came from the jungle. Souho, the hunter, threw himself flat on the ground. His hands had grabbed the most powerful gun.

This was a .450 Express, a British model. Souho exploded the big-game killer. But its high-velocity bullets only clipped leaves from the jungle where no one seemed to be moving.

Renny came out with a clumsy looking weapon. It was a superfire machine pistol, loaded with a drum of quick-firing bullets. The pistol made a noise like an immense bullfiddle. But its slugs only mowed a path a little to one side of where the carrier boys were running.

Perhaps most of the score of native boys had been killed. The others had slithered away. Renny muttered grimly.

"Holy cow!" boomed Renny. "If I could only get an eye on some of them devils!"

While the guns were whooping and banging, no more spears had fallen. If three boys had not been lying transfixed by the murderous blades, it would have seemed there had been no attack.

This was amazing. The tribal warriors usually accompany their attacks with much shouting.

Chapter II

WHITE MAN'S VOICE

ONLY Souho and Mapanda had remained with Renny. The big engineer ordered them behind the tents. A faint moaning came from the jungle bush.

Renny judged this must be one of his carrier boys. He was about to investigate, when Souho interfered.

"Masai make some trick, *b'wana*," he warned. "Him be Juju voice. Most good stay now."

Renny, always ready for an open scrap, was somewhat bewildered. He listened carefully. Souho's warning had been well judged. The moaning voice was not that of a man in pain.

Renny started to pull away the body of the dead carrier closest to the fire. A whistling wind fanned his head. A long spear, ornamented with red-dyed ostrich feathers, jammed its blade into the ground.

Around the haft of the spear a white paper was tied. Renny unrolled the white paper. There was a note printed in English:

COLONEL RENWICK MUST LEAVE THIS LAND AT ONCE. THE RAILROAD WILL NEVER BE BUILT. THIS WILL BE THE ONLY WARNING.

"So there is a white man mixed up in this," growled Renny. "That poor devil they got was right. This is something Doc must know at once!"

Renny whipped back toward his tent. He twisted the dials of the radio transmitter.

Possible the leader of the natives concealed in the jungle had never seen a radio broadcast from so small an instrument. Renny started speaking. Almost at once, a low but penetrating voice replied.

"Doc speaking, Renny. I can hear you clearly."

The voice of Doc Savage never was raised. It had a peculiar timbre, a great carrying quality.

"Doc, there's trouble breaking over here!" boomed Renny. "The richest region in Central Africa is about to be invaded. King Udu of Kokoland sent six runners to me. Only one arrived, and he was dying."

Souho gripped Renny's arm. The hunter raised the heavy express rifle. He was pointing it at the thick foliage beyond the fire. More than leaves had suddenly appeared. Red ostrich plumes suddenly marked the green wall.

"Don't shoot!" snapped Renny, catching Souho's arm.

"Doc—I've gotta talk fast—I've been ordered out—this King Udu has a son, Prince Zaban, in New York—the kingdom is about to be overthrown!"

GUTTURAL, snarling cries came from the bush. A fantastic figure dressed in the hide and the mane of a lion, leaped into the circle of the fire. Souho's rifle exploded.

One of the red blotches came from the wall. A huge warrior with a red ostrich headdress slammed on his face.

"They're on top of us, Doc!" roared Renny. "King Udu has sent men to guard his son in New York—one of his former subjects lives there—he is called Logo—King Udu has sent him a—"

Spears hissed across the fire. Renny paused to pull the transmitter out of immediate range of the spears.

"What did King Udu send?" came Doc's clear voice.

"King Udu has sent the kingdom's royal—"

Souho roared with pain. The haft of a spear had struck him over one ear. Two luridly painted warriors sprang from between the tents. They were dragging Mapanda between them.

"Holy cow, Doc!" shouted Renny. "See Prince Zaban—he'll know—the Long Juju has—"

Renny was completely ringed by the attackers. In the language of the Masai, a white man's voice emanated from the lion's head.

"Seize him! Break up that box!"

Half a dozen warriors hurled themselves back of the tents.

Renny heaved to his feet. He was suddenly facing a ring of long-bladed spears.

"If you are wise," said the lion-clad man in English, "you will not resist. We want only that you should forget this crazy railroad and leave the country."

"Not in a thousand years!" bellowed the enraged engineer.

He sprang between two of the spear blades. One fist, many pounds in weight, mangled the headdress of the nearest warrior into his skull.

Renny hurled himself straight toward the English-speaking leader. He saw only what looked like the shadow of some flying object. A war club covered with painted knobs cracked across the back of Renny's thick neck. As he fell, Renny let out one thunderous roar. He was close to the radio transmitter.

RENNY's yell traveled a few thousand miles. It roared from the loud-speaker of a radio board on the wall of Doc Savage's laboratory in the heart of Manhattan.

The man before the radio was bigger than the huge Renny. He did not appear to be as big, due to the symmetry of his massive figure. The skin of his face and of his hands and bared forearms was of the smoothest golden bronze. His hair fitted closely to his skull. Its color seemed almost a continuation of his skin.

At Renny's yell, a childlike voice spoke anxiously.

"Howlin' calamities, Doc! Now Renny's gone an' got himself into some sure enough trouble!"

The speaker could easily have been mistaken for a dressed gorilla. Red, furry hair covered all of his visible parts.

"Looks that way, Monk," stated Doc quietly. "Undoubtedly we have just been listening to an attack of warriors in the heart of an African jungle."

"African jungle?" crackled a dry, sarcastic voice. "Now, that's right up Monk's alley. Maybe if we go to Africa, we'll succeed in leaving him with his kinfolks!"

This speaker was an elegantly clad, waspish-waisted man. His face was thin and his eyes were keen.

"Dag-gonit, Ham!" squeaked the hairy one. "Renny's in a jam, an' you go makin' shyster jokes that don't mean nothin'!"

"Renny's probably having the time of his life," observed Ham.

"Ham," Theodore Marley Brooks, was the legal luminary of Doc Savage's group. He was one of the country's smartest lawyers.

"Monk" was Andrew Blodgett Mayfair, noted industrial chemist. Monk was still glaring at Ham. Doc ignored their dispute.

"It is to be regretted Renny was unable to inform us what King Udu has probably sent to New York," said the bronze man. "First, we shall have to make contact with this Prince Zaban, if he happens to be in Manhattan."

"Renny said this African potentate has sent men to New York," said Ham. "An' that fellow he called Logo? Maybe we could find him. The only trouble is, he's likely living over in Harlem under the name of Brown or Smith or something."

"You are possibly correct," said Doc Savage. "However, I believe we shall learn something of Prince Zaban in a very short time. This King Udu is old, but he is a remarkably well-informed ruler. He is king over nearly forty different tribes, some of them wild, but his own race seems to have sprung from an early invasion of the Kilimanjaro country by the ancient Romans."

Doc Savage and his men were to hear news of Prince Zaban very soon. For, as the man of bronze discovered all further effort to contact Renny was useless, two groups of strange, dark-skinned men were approaching the towering skyscraper.

Brilliant morning sunshine afforded an unusual atmosphere for the grim tragedy which was closely impending.

A uniformed messenger was hurrying along one of the narrow streets. This thoroughfare converged with another at the intersection above which the glittering skyscraper reared its tower.

On this intersecting street was another messenger. This was not unusual, but each of these messengers was swarthy of skin, and each had a thinly boned, arching nose. Each hurrying man carried a package wrapped in heavy manila paper.

A short distance behind each messenger, half a dozen or more men threaded their way through the dense crowds. They, too, were of dark skin. These men wore the turbans of native Hindus of India. Yet any observer would have noted these men were not Hindus.

The noses of all these men were flat and very broad. Their turbans were tightly wrapped. The folds of cloth concealed their ears.

One messenger carried his package under his arm. He had nearly reached the street intersection. Turbaned men suddenly shoved other pedestrians aside and sprang toward the messenger.

A woman emitted a scream. One of the turbaned men had torn the package from under the messenger's arm. Another clamped his hands on the messenger's throat.

Four or five wearing the turbans had blocked off others on the sidewalk. Smart pedestrians sprang away. A husky, Irish traffic policeman let out a shrill alarm from his whistle. He had seen the beginning of the attack.

The copper had his gun in his hand. He yelled, "Hey! Get 'em up, you devils, before I blast yuh!"

Perhaps the traffic officer saw an opportunity to cover himself with glory. No weapons showed in the hands of any of the turbaned men.

The turbaned men ignored the policeman's order. The one who had seized the package, ripped off the manila covering. The object inside looked like a solid block of polished wood.

The turbaned man let out a yell of triumph. The man in the messenger's uniform had ceased to resist. A queer smile played suddenly over his face.

That smile was his last. It was a sardonic grin. Possibly it should have warned the men who had seized him.

The man holding the strange block fumbled his fingers along one edge. This man was almost completely obliterated. The block exploded with a terrific impact. The blast ripped open a small crater in the sidewalk.

THE traffic policeman's revolver exploded in the grip of a hand that probably was already dead. A score of persons were hurled onto the sidewalk and into the building where plate glass was shattered.

In the intersecting street, the attack of turbaned men upon the other messenger had been almost simultaneous with the terrible explosion. This messenger put up a fierce fight.

No weapons were used. But two of the turbaned men were knocked down before one wrested the package from their victim. Then one of the attackers struck the messenger with what appeared to be a small, pointed dart.

The messenger's nostrils dilated. He emitted a strange, terrible laugh. The heavy paper was being torn from another object that was apparently only a block of solid wood.

The polished oblong gave forth a hissing. The turbaned man holding it crumpled to the sidewalk. The block struck and burst into flames.

Five men wearing the peculiar turbans fell down. One clawed madly at his eyes. It pulled the turban loose. Parts of his ears seemed to fall away. But they were still attached. They were the lobes of the ears, horribly distorted into great rings of flesh.

All of the men who fell died almost instantly. Close to the ashes of the oblong block lay the messenger who had carried it. Across his lips was a sardonic grin. A small dart protruded from his neck.

Radio police cars and ambulances screamed into the two blocks. Nothing remained of either of the oblong packages. It was plainly evident one had been packed with high explosive.

It was equally evident the other had been the container of some deadly, instantly effective gas.

A captain of detectives found a small piece of manila paper intact. He stared at it.

"You might have known he would have something to do with this!" he growled. "Joe, have headquarters get in touch with Doc Savage!"

On the salvaged bit of heavy paper was the name *CLARK SAVAGE JR*. The package had been sealed with a blue wax. Where this had been broken appeared the imprint of a curious seal.

The small figure in this seal was grotesquely ugly.

Chapter III

THE SEALED BOX

IF the white messenger bearing a third package had known of the first two, he might not have so jauntily entered the elevator in the glittering skyscraper.

The tragic explosion took place while he was shooting toward the eighty-sixth floor. Arriving at the eighty-sixth floor the messenger was directed to Doc Savage's door.

Almost immediately the messenger became somewhat dizzy. He had walked over to a door that looked like a panel in the wall. It had neither lock, knob nor latch. Clark Savage, Jr., appeared in small bronze letters.

Before the messenger could reach for the buzzer, the door opened silently. The fuzzy, ugly face of Monk glowered at the visitor. Monk reached for the package.

"Gimme your book an' I'll sign for it," said Monk.

"Got to deliver this personal to Mr. Savage," said the messenger. "He's got to see me!"

"Yeah?" piped Monk. "He's already seen you. I'll take it."

A hand at the end of an incredibly long arm flipped the package from the messenger's hands.

"You'll stand right here!" snapped Monk. "An' don't move!"

Monk's foot did something to the thick rug of the big reception room. The messenger heard nothing. The door by which he had entered was no longer in evidence. He was looking at a smooth, unbroken wall.

Monk carried the package through the library with its thousands of scientific and other books, into the laboratory. Doc Savage turned from the radio.

"There seems no doubt but they've got Renny," he stated. "I have called Johnny. He will know the whereabouts of Prince Zaban."

"JOHNNY" was William Harper Littlejohn, geologist and archæologist. When strange visitors came to Manhattan, Johnny nearly always made contact with them.

Monk shifted the oblong package in his hairy hands. The manila paper covering was sealed with blobs of blue wax.

In each of these seals was a grotesque miniature. It had somewhat the shape of a scorpion.

Monk started to tear off the paper. Ham caught the package.

"Wait a minute, insect," snapped the lawyer. "Probably that package is for Doc."

"Yeah, sure," said Monk. "I was just goin' to open it."

Doc Savage's flaky gold eyes were fixed on the parcel. In those eyes life stirred like the movement of small whirlpools.

The big laboratory was suddenly filled with a fantastic sound. It was a low, mellow trilling, as if a wind were playing over reed instruments.

Monk hastily deposited the package on a table. Doc's trilling sound seemed to emanate from his whole body. Sometimes it warned of impending danger. At others it announced the bronze man was on the eve of a discovery.

"Leave the package untouched for a moment," advised Doc. "I have seen the messenger. He seems to be from a regular agency. We will investigate."

In a few seconds the agency was on the telephone. In the reception room the puzzled messenger was in somewhat of a daze. He walked along the wall which he believed to be facing the outside corridor. He ran his hands along its smooth surface.

"It's dog-goned screwy," he muttered. "I know that door's right here somewhere."

Another door of chrome steel leading into the library had been closed by Monk. The messenger was temporarily a prisoner.

Doc SAVAGE finished his talk with the messenger agency.

"The package was left with the agency less than half an hour ago for delivery here," announced Doc. "It was brought in by a colored man in a chauffeur's uniform. He said it was important this be delivered at once."

The man of bronze inspected the oblong package carefully. The whirlpools stirred again in his flaky gold eyes as he studied the seal in blue.

It was not odd that the only address was Clark Savage, Jr. In the upper left-hand corner was printed with ink a return address:

WILLIAM SMITH
4404 Crooked Neck Road, Long Island

"That isn't in Harlem," observed Ham, "but I mentioned this fellow Logo probably would be living under the name of Smith or something near it."

"That might be," stated Doc. "But if this should develop into what Renny was trying to inform us about, it is a most remarkable coincidence that it should arrive just now."

Doc Savage took the oblong package in his hands.

The man of bronze stripped the manila paper carefully away. He was holding what appeared to be a solid block of polished teakwood.

If there was a hollow space inside, the craftsmanship of the maker had left not so much as a hair line in the fine-grained wood.

"I would proceed with extraordinary caution, Doc," suddenly spoke a calm voice behind the bronze man. "As nearly as I have assimilated the facts, that package resembles two others that have just killed a dozen persons."

Johnny had appeared abruptly. The archæologist had come from a sliding panel concealed by a glass tank filled with tropical fish.

Doc replaced the oblong block on the table. Johnny told of the weird tragedies.

"You say some of the men who were killed had deformed ears with extended lobes," stated Doc. "The Masai and the Waperri of Central Africa are among the tribes having that practice. The man who carried one of the boxes had a lighter skin and an arching nose. That would make him one of the Kokonese."

"Indubitably," observed Johnny, who was addicted to long words. "I judged the dead men to be omophagous Ulotrichans. They are likely to demonstrate they can be as poisonous as the Proterogluphya."

"Howlin' calamities!" squeaked Monk. "They couldn't possibly be that bad!"

"Yes," smiled Doc. "Those tribes do eat raw flesh and they would have woolly hair. Some are as deadly as cobras."

Doc's bronze hands played along the edges of the oblong block. The block had weight that indicated it might indeed be solid. Yet the man of bronze was convinced something was contained inside.

"Perhaps it would be well not to employ force," Doc stated. "We will lock this away for the present."

He placed the polished oblong block carefully in the strong safe.

IN the other room the nonplused messenger tried whistling.

"I don't care if this guy is Doc Savage," he complained. "He can't make a monkey outta me!"

He did not hear the step of Monk behind him.

"There ain't anything holdin' you," said the ugly-looking chemist.

"Oh, yeah?" rapped the messenger. "And how the——"

He gulped and looked at the outer wall. Monk had stepped on something under the rug. The messenger was looking at the door which led to the outside.

There was the corridor. Directly opposite were the elevators. The lock was operated by an invisible electroscope.

"Good gosh!" howled the messenger. "I don't like any of this shenanigans! Where's that door been?"

"The door hasn't moved," stated Monk.

The messenger was beginning to believe he had been seeing things. A smoothly moving panel had made a false wall over the door.

Doc Savage had found it convenient at times to prevent some of his many visitors from finding their way out too quickly.

The messenger breathed a sigh of relief when the elevator's doors closed behind his back. He had been glad to get away.

BACK in the laboratory, Doc Savage was summoned to the telephone. It was the commissioner of police.

"Whatever you do, Mr. Savage, don't accept or open any packages!" said the commissioner. "Hell seems to have broken loose! Unless I'm crazy, somebody is trying to move an African war right into Manhattan! You've heard of the explosion?"

"I have just been informed of the regrettable facts," stated Doc.

"Well, your name was on the paper around the infernal

machine that went off first!" said the commissioner. "Have you had any recent dealings with a bunch of heathen that runs around with their ears hanging down to their shoulders?"

"I have had no contacts of that character," stated Doc truthfully. "Perhaps some one was trying to reach me."

"Yes!" rapped the commissioner. "And there must have been two of them, for that other box burned up! Maybe it had your address, too!"

"It might be," stated Doc. "I shall see what I can ascertain and keep you informed of anything that may aid the police."

"I'll let you know if anything more turns up," said the commissioner. "We've had a report of some funny dark fellows that seem to be camping out over in the Crooked Neck section of Long Island."

Doc turned to his three companions. Another of his men, Major Thomas J. Roberts, known as "Long Tom," the electrician of the group, was attending a convention on the Pacific coast.

"I have no doubt," stated Doc, "but all of this may be connected with King Udu and Kokoland. King Udu probably has sent some of his most loyal subjects to this country. The block of teakwood we have received may or may not be all right."

"But those others, Doc?" said Ham.

"We will take all necessary precautions," advised Doc. "But I imagine the enemies of King Udu are even now in New York. If this is true, the first two packages may have been a deliberate decoy of death, while a similar box was being delivered to us."

"Dag-gonit!" complained Monk. "It looks like a lot of monkey business to me!"

"And who would know more about monkey business than a human ape," grinned Ham. "If we do have to go to Africa, we'll be busy keeping you out of the trees."

"You'll be plenty busy keepin' me from pattin' the ground on your shyster face!" howled Monk.

"Johnny, we should make immediate contact with Prince Zaban of Kokoland," announced Doc. "You know something of his royal highness and where he might be?"

"Prince Zaban is stopping at the Adirondack Hotel. He is one of the few royal princes of a long family line. Educated at Oxford. Apparently he has been sent to America to absorb some of our modern ideas."

"Then he has a retinue of his own servants?" said Doc.

"No," replied Johnny. "The prince is accompanied by a former Oxford student, a Count Cardoti. Count Cardoti seems to have become his patron in this country. He has arranged several public appearances. The prince is to speak before one of the archaeological societies to-night."

"Count Cardoti could then be of the Spanish race," said Doc.

"Apparently, though that is somewhat obscure," said Johnny. "The count is a polished fellow. But he has spent a number of years in the Taveta country of Africa."

Doc Savage made one more attempt to pick up the distant radio transmitter of Renny. There was no response.

"I believe Renny has been made a prisoner," stated Doc. "He probably will be safe for some time. Those behind the trouble in the Kilimanjaro country would hardly want to become involved with the United States. We will get in contact with Prince Zaban."

Doc's call to the Adirondack Hotel was connected with the suite of Prince Zaban. There was no reply.

"I don't understand why they don't answer," said the girl at the switchboard. "I am sure they are in. There were some visitors went up quite a while ago, and they are still there."

Doc Savage whipped from the telephone. The trill of danger was emanating from the bronze man.

"Johnny," he directed, "you will come with me at once. We may be too late. Ham, you and Monk, stay here. Be careful whom you admit. I would not be surprised if you would have some visitors."

Doc did not explain why he expected visitors.

WHEN Doc Savage and Johnny arrived at the hotel, police cars were lined up at the curb. Johnny gasped. Grimly, Doc led the way to Prince Zaban's suite. More police, reporters, and a jabbering hotel manager were crowded about the door to the royal prince's suite. Doc Savage elbowed his way inside. And then the odd trilling sound came from his lips.

"I was afraid of this," he said grimly.

Police officers and reporters stepped back as Doc moved forward to take a glimpse of the motionless figure on the expensive rug. A short stubby arrow, cruelly barbed, had been jammed deep into Prince Zaban's throat. Red Ostrich feathers were affixed to the haft of the arrow. The life blood of Prince Zaban had gushed out in a stream. It was not a pretty sight.

Count Cardoti lurched through the group to Doc Savage's side. The count looked white and stricken. He was choked with grief as he recounted what had happened.

"It was four Negro porters!" he cried. "They forced their way in here as I was admitting two newspapermen. But they weren't really porters. They were Africans! They were Jujus!—and they tried to make Prince Zaban tell them the location of the Blood Idol."

Two reporters crowded forward. "What is the Blood Idol?" demanded one.

"I'm sure I cannot tell you," said Count Cardoti. "There are many tribal gods and fetishes in Central East Africa. I only know that my poor friend feared some evil was about to overtake his father, King Udu."

"You have been a friend of Prince Zaban?" questioned Doc Savage.

"Since he was a small boy," said Count Cardoti sadly. "Prince Zaban was like a younger brother."

Policemen were reporting. The zone around the Adirondack Hotel had been blocked in. Down on the street a woman had fainted. Revived, she had screamed, "His ears! Those terrible ears!"

The police learned she had seen four Africans drive away in a fast car. She had not seen the license number. But she believed the car had turned toward the Queensboro Bridge across the East River.

Doc Savage said to Johnny, "There may be more in that Long Island address than we think."

"This dead man," stated the medical examiner, "seems to be of a peculiar type. You tell me he is an African? It is strange."

The erudite Johnny spoke.

"Centuries ago the land of Kilimanjaro was raided by a lost legion of the ancient Romans under Cæsar," he stated. "These raiders never returned to their own country. You see the results of a mingling of the races in the distant past."

"That is true, I believe," said Count Cardoti. "And my friend was the direct successor to the throne of King Udu. He was the only living heir."

Doc Savage said quietly, "When you have finished here, Count Cardoti, will you come to my headquarters?"

LEFT together in Doc Savage's headquarters, Monk and Ham were, as usual, apparently about to murder each other.

"You'll keep that filthy, misfit quadruped off my coat or I'll make shark bait of him!" rasped Ham.

"You touch that pig and there won't be enough shyster lawyer left to feed the sharks!" howled Monk.

The subject of this virulent discourse waved his long ears. He was Habeas Corpus, the Australian bush hog which Monk had adopted as his special pet.

Habeas Corpus was a wise pig. He was only a few slats of ribs put together on ludicrously long legs.

Habeas Corpus suddenly was forgotten. The telephone buzzed. Each of the sparring companions got to an instrument. The voice that spoke was another point of keenest rivalry between them.

The speaker was Patricia Savage, the beautiful and talented cousin of the famous Doc. She was talking from her beauty parlor and physical culture institution just off Park Avenue.

"I must find Doc as soon as possible," announced Pat Savage.

"You sound excited, Pat," replied Ham. "What's happened?"

"I can't tell you—but I want Doc to come over—I can't say any more from here—but it's important—tell Doc—no, wait! It's too late—I'll—I'll call back!"

The connection was cut off abruptly. But not quick enough to drown out a woman's scream.

"Howlin' calamities!" exploded Monk. "Somebody's done something to Pat! Come on!"

Ham was a little more calm.

"That wasn't Pat's voice yelled," he advised. "Besides, Pat never screamed in her life."

"I ain't wastin' any time!" howled Monk.

Ham apparently decided Pat was more important than waiting for possible visitors. He was with Monk as Doc's special high-speed elevator dropped them. The pair made a dash for the garage underground.

Chapter IV

THE BLACK HIDE-OUT

MONK and Ham knew nothing of the assassination of Prince Zaban. At the time they arrived at Pat Savage's establishment, Doc Savage was returning to his headquarters.

Count Cardoti had convinced the police of his genuine grief over the death of the prince. He readily accepted Doc's suggestion that he accompany him. Apparently Count Cardoti knew something of the bronze man's reputation.

"If any person on earth can run these assassins to earth, you can do it," he stated to Doc.

About this time Ham and Monk were interviewing Margaret, Pat's assistant at the beauty shop. She could furnish only one lead.

"Miss Savage got into a car with Señorita Moncarid," she told Ham and Monk. "The señorita was here getting a facial. Then four Negroes came here and she was terrified. She asked Miss Savage to take her to a hotel. The four men followed them in a big car, although Miss Savage had the señorita disguised in a blond wig and a different coat."

"Anything else?" prompted Ham.

"Well, this señorita—" exclaimed the assistant, "I don't think she's Spanish. She had funny ears, and a little thing like a scorpion tattoed on her shoulder. She said something in an odd language when she saw the Negroes."

"Dag-gonit!" complained Monk. "I'll bet Pat's got herself into a real jam!"

"Yeah," drawled Ham, "and she probably thinks she's having the time of her life. I'm calling this señorita's hotel."

"I hope Pat went there." said Monk.

Ham's face clouded. He was on the phone. He said, "Yes, all right," and hung up.

"It seems Pat must be all right," he said in a relieved voice. "She is with this Señorita Moncarid. The señorita had called her hotel. She left an address if any one called inquiring for Pat. It's on the upper East Side."

HAM and Monk drove rapidly to the East Side address. They surveyed the gloomy warehouse and loft building.

"Betcha the whole thing's a trap!" complained Monk. "Maybe we oughtta call up Doc!"

Ham vetoed wasting any time. Descending from the car, he walked toward the partly open door of the deserted warehouse.

"But there've been a couple of cars here not long ago," said Ham, pointing to the tire marks in the dust. "They've been inside."

The lean lawyer flourished his smooth black cane and stepped inside the doorway. Monk lumbered after him. The interior of the warehouse was too dark to give a view more than a few feet.

Ham kicked around disgustedly. He was careful not to soil his trousers and coat.

Tracks showed many feet had trampled in the dust.

Ham poked his black cane into the dust. That cane was a dangerous weapon. It sheathed the finest steel blade with a tip drugged to put an enemy out of business.

Monk let out a yell and dropped to his hands and knees. He scurried around like some furry gorilla.

"I thought you'd go that way some time," drawled Ham sarcastically. "Now what do you think you're looking for?"

"Pat was here!" shouted Monk. "I'd know her feet in a million! Hey! Look at this!"

Monk heaved to his feet. He was clutching Pat's small automatic pistol.

"Dag-gonnit!" he yelped. "She's put up a fight! Maybe she's still upstairs somewhere!"

They listened for a few seconds. The only sound was a rat gnawing wood. The place was ghostly.

Ham found a door leading to a stairway. The narrow entrance was opaque. He preceded Monk through the door. Then he yelled out a rare oath.

"Hey, you danged shyster!" squealed Monk. "Where'd you think you're goin'?"

HAM had seemed to perform a queer, acrobatic feat. He had leaped straight up. One of his flying heels rapped Monk's ugly chin.

"Dag-gone you!" exploded Monk, making a grab for the foot.

Monk's long arm remained extended. His short legs were jerked from under him. He made a short, breath-taking flight that ended in a jouncing jolt.

"Hey, lemme go!" he yelled.

Ham's body banged against him in the darkness. Monk slapped out with one fist. Ham kicked at him.

The feet of both men dangled several feet from the floor. They were being bounced gently up and down. Loops tightened around their bodies.

Near by sounded a rush of feet. Monk let out a whoop and produced his superfire pistol. The warehouse seemed suddenly to be filled with a million bees.

Monk sprayed mercy bullets at random. Hoarse voices squawked. Ham had loosened his sword blade. He punched at shadows. Then a light flashed. Monk and Ham were ringed in by dark faces. They saw dancing heads with grotesque ears. A dozen short swords slashed at their feet.

Ham flicked back with his long blade. Two attackers suddenly fell, knocked out by Ham's sword.

Monk got four or five men with mercy bullets. These would keep them asleep for a couple of hours.

Ham attempted to loosen the thing that had caught them. It was a device such as might have been found in the jungle. Pieces of steel had been bent and fitted with slipnooses. Ham and Monk had walked into these loops.

They were held off the floor as wild animals might have been lifted on some tropical water trail.

Monk's superfirer and Ham's sword set the Africans back for a moment. They went into a huddle. Ham started to slice the loop around him with his sword blade.

But the lawyer did not complete his escape. He gave a shout of warning.

"Drop your pistol, Monk, or we're done for!"

Ham let his sword blade clatter to the floor. Monk gave one look at the near-by men and his superfirer thudded after the sword.

Two men had stepped forward. They were holding what might have been bean-shooters. The tubes pointed at Ham and Monk.

"We give up!" yelled Ham. "Hold up on that stuff!"

Whether or not the Africans understood, they lowered the short tubes. Ham had instantly recognized the bean-shooters as deadly blowpipes of the African jungle.

The jabbering men lowered Ham and Monk. They enwrapped them with long strips of rattan. Monk gurgled over the chunk of evil-tasting wax thrust into his mouth.

The Africans carried their prisoners up three flights of stairs. They dumped them into a room.

Monk and Ham at first thought it was empty. Neither could speak. There was a shuffling on the floor. A little light came through a dirty window.

Pat Savage lay there blinking at them. She made gurgling noises in her throat.

Ham's hands were secured behind him. He began thumping with his heels. The thumps were unevenly spaced. Pat Savage's small heels also thumped. This was an abbreviation of the Morse code devised by Doc Savage.

"Where is Señorita Moncarid?" was Ham's message.

"Believe she is boss of these men," thumped Pat.

"Knew it," tapped Ham. "She trapped us. It is scheme to get Doc. Sent him infernal machine. He has it in safe."

The Africans appeared to have gone to another part of the building. Ham attempted to cut his rattan bindings with a keen blade which sprang from the inside of a signet ring on his right hand.

But the tough, bark fibre of the jungle could not be severed.

AT about the time Ham was telling Pat Savage of the supposed infernal machine in Doc's safe, the man of bronze was ascending to his headquarters. Count Cardoti exclaimed as Doc Savage's door opened without being touched.

Inside the door, Doc Savage halted abruptly. From him came the mellow, fantastic trilling. He lifted his hand as a signal for Johnny and Count Cardoti to proceed with caution.

"We have had visitors," he announced quietly.

The bronze man had glanced at one of the wall panels.

This panel contained several dials. A red needle was slowly vibrating.

This informed Doc that one of several secret entrances had been disturbed.

"What do you suppose has happened to Ham and Monk?" questioned Johnny. "They were to stay here."

Doc Savage whipped through the library into the inner room. Count Cardoti and Johnny followed closely.

Count Cardoti let out a surprised oath.

"I can't understand what has caused this visit in force to America," he added. "Good grief, Mr. Savage! They have had a death battle right here in your place!"

Count Cardoti had spoken correctly. Huge glass retorts and scores of small glass containers had been shattered.

Two dead men lay in front of the huge safe. The door of the safe had been deeply gouged with steel instruments. But the invaders had not succeeded in gaining an entrance.

"They're Masai or Waperri," said Count Cardoti. "They are of the same tribe that killed Prince Zaban. Their ears are the same."

The dead men's ear lobes were loops of deformed flesh.

"Again we seem to have the arrow of the red ostrich," stated Doc. "That is the war sign of the Masai."

"That offers a strange contradiction," stated Johnny. "Unless they have started killing each other."

Arrows were stuck into the throats of the dead men.

"I imagine," stated Doc, "these men were not killed by their own tribesmen. Their own arrows were used as murder weapons."

Count Cardoti bent over two small glasses on the floor beside the bodies. Each was filled with blood. Undoubtedly it had been drawn from the veins of the two dead men.

Count Cardoti's face was gray and pinched. His black eyes glittered.

"It is strange," he announced. "Here is evidence there must be a considerable number of Kokonese in New York. Neither the prince nor myself knew of their presence. The glasses of blood tell it."

"The Kokonese are not blood-drinkers," stated Doc.

"That's just it," replied Count Cardoti. "The Masai and the Waperri do drink the blood of their enemies. So, when they are killed by the Kokonese, the victors often leave a vessel of their own blood. It is a gesture of contempt."

"These aborigines seem to be very pleasant people," commented Johnny. "What do you suppose happened to Ham and Monk?"

Doc Savage did not reply. He had produced a small cylinder. A pressure of a button set a generator buzzing. The man of bronze moved with apparent aimlessness across the laboratory.

But when Doc halted, one foot was pressing a spring concealed under the edge of a table. He pointed the gleaming cylinder at the big safe. The tumblers of the lock slid back noiselessly.

The ponderous door swung open.

The block of polished teakwood reposed inside. Count Cardoti had been staring at the opening of the safe. He associated the unlocking with the buzzing cylinder in Doc's hand.

The cylinder had no connection with the apparent magic. It was a ruse sometimes employed by the bronze man when he desired to open the safe in the presence of visitors.

Doc had already informed Count Cardoti something of the tragedies of the early morning. The police had mentioned them. Not until now had the man of bronze made any reference to his own teakwood package.

"Good grief!" exploded Count Cardoti. "This is like the infernal machines on the street! Where did it come from?"

"It was delivered by a special messenger this morning," stated Doc.

The count's pointed face became the color of wax.

"I thought I would keep it and see what happened," said Doc calmly. "If it is an infernal machine, these men would hardly have been so eager to obtain possession of it."

Count Cardoti's face lighted a little. He nodded.

"I had not thought of that," he admitted. "Still, I think it is dangerous. Have you opened it?"

"Perhaps you might suggest some way it could be done," stated Doc unexpectedly. "I know now it has come from some of these tribal factions. Have you ever seen anything resembling it?"

"Never," declared Count Cardoti.

Doc's bronzed hands slid over the polished surface as if seeking for some hidden spring.

"Please, Mr. Savage, I wouldn't attempt to open it, if it

can be opened," said Count Cardoti. "I admit since what happened to Prince Zaban my nerves are on edge."

"Perhaps that is good advice," said Doc. "We will leave it for the present."

HE returned the teakwood block to the safe.

Without explanation, Doc suddenly glided into the library. When he emerged in the outer room, he carried a square black box. Its lens gave it the appearance of an old-fashioned stereoscope.

No light came from the lens, but when it was pointed at the window of the outside room, glowing words leaped into view.

The beam was the ultra-violet or black light. The words had been written with a substance which fluoresced under this invisible ray. The message had been left by Ham:

PAT POSSIBLY IN TROUBLE. WE HAVE GONE THERE.

Doc whipped instantly to the telephone. His brief conversation with Pat's establishment brought the only facts they had.

Pat Savage had disappeared with a mysterious dark woman calling herself Señorita Moncarid. There had been an invasion of Africans. Monk and Ham had received a message from the señorita's hotel. They had gone to find Pat.

Doc immediately called the hotel named. No. There had been no further word from Señorita Moncarid. Only she had left some message for any one seeking Pat Savage.

"Wait a minute," said the hotel operator. In a few seconds she added, "The message was delivered. The girl who was on the board before me destroyed the address it gave. Now she has gone to Coney Island."

Doc's fantastic trilling broke out. He was convinced that Pat was in serious danger.

SEÑORITA MONCARID was a new angle. In what manner could she be connected with the fantastic tribal warfare?

The man of bronze analyzed the whole situation quickly.

King Udu of Kokoland had sought to safeguard Prince Zaban in New York. In some manner, his subjects had failed. There had been the apparent deliberate decoying of enemy

Masai warriors to their deaths in the explosion and by the other flaming package.

Then the teakwood block had come to Doc Savage.

Doc whipped back into the laboratory. Picking up the paper wrapping which had been around the package, he studied the address again:

WILLIAM SMITH
4404 Crooked Neck Road, Long Island

Doc got on the telephone. The commissioner of police replied.

"No," said the commissioner, "we have been unable to get anything definite on Long Island. Some farmers living on Crooked Neck Road in Long Island have reported strange Negro men in the vicinity. But the place is almost a wilderness."

"I know," stated Doc. "The region is in upper Suffolk County. For the most part the land there consists of sandy barrens."

The man of bronze thumbed through a Long Island directory. He put his finger on Crooked Neck Road. There was no definite address of 4404, and there was no name of William Smith.

Despite the evident falseness of the address, Doc announced to the others, "I believe we may discover something of importance on Long Island. We should arrive there shortly after sunset."

Chapter V

DEAD MEN SIT UP

PERHAPS Count Cardoti got a kick out of being with Doc Savage. He certainly found no dull moment.

A night motor ride with Doc on Long Island had its thrills.

His supermotor, silenced to a whisper, shot the bulletproof sedan over a series of back roads.

The bronze man drove, as he did everything else, with greatest concentration. Twice motor-cycle cops started to pick up the car. Then they dropped back.

Doc Savage carried a police commission. When he hit seventy miles an hour, it must be serious business. The big car threaded the most dangerous traffic.

"If I knew more of the tribal affairs of Kokoland I might be of greater assistance," said Count Cardoti when they were flying along a quiet road. "King Udu's people are mysterious. His family has ruled forty or more of the wildest tribes through some tradition. The crown must be passed on to a direct descendant. This descendant is obliged to be in possession of some tribal or family fetish."

"Perhaps analogous to an escutcheon or the emblazonment of some individual armorial bearings," suggested the long-worded Johnny. "In Africa, this may be some trivial object such as a feather, a weapon or an odd stone."

"I am not aware what it might be," stated Count Cardoti. "As it developed, when my poor friend was so brutally killed, the Masai seemed to be seeking something the prince called the Blood Idol."

"Had you known of trouble being fomented in King Udu's empire?" said Doc Savage.

"Ever since I have known these tribes, there has been dissension," said Count Cardoti. "But King Udu has been a good ruler. The great fear of Kokoland has been the greed of some outside power. Their land is wonderfully rich."

"And the assassination of the prince removes the last of the direct heirs to the throne?" questioned Doc.

"Yes," declared Count Cordoti. "King Udu had only two children. One, the sister of Prince Zaban, was killed by the Masai in an outbreak when she was about four years old. The death of my poor friend throws his country wide open to rebellion and conquest of outside powers."

"So I had judged," stated Doc. "It becomes apparent we should visit the land of the Kokonese."

Count Cardoti's intense black eyes lighted.

"You would permit me to accompany you on such a mission?" he ventured.

"I should expect you to do so, as your knowledge of the land may prove valuable," advised Doc.

"Good enough," exclaimed Count Cardoti. "I am pleased."

THE car's headlights bored a white tunnel along a straggling road. A white corner post bore the name: "CROOKED NECK ROAD." The car slid into the narrow lane.

The land all about seemed to be poor. Larger trees had given way to scrubby brush. Open fields appeared.

"The terrain hardly seems conducive to habitation," commented Johnny. "There seems to be an absence of domiciliary structures."

"There are a few scattered farms," stated Doc. "There is a small red house just beyond the bend, half a mile ahead."

The bronze man's knowledge of little known roads was astounding. A button flicked out the headlights. Count Cardoti gasped.

"You might try the effect of these," suggested Doc.

What appeared to be oversized goggles were thrust into Count Cardoti's hands. Johnny was putting on a similar pair. Doc also had donned the goggles.

"Why, it makes everything like a black-and-white cinema," said Count Cardoti. "I can see more plainly than with the other light."

"The infra-red beam," explained Johnny. "It is invisible to the unassisted optic, but provides an etching of high-lights when picked up by the lenses."

The house Doc had mentioned was around the bend of the road. The big car whispered into the stretch. Doc abruptly braked to a noiseless stop.

A black-and-white panorama had flashed into view. And the scene spelled trouble. The double blast of a shotgun shattered the night.

"We have a strange faculty for arriving at the psychological interim," observed Johnny dryly. "It seems we need not journey to darkest Africa to discover violent conflict."

"Good grief!" exploded Count Cardoti. "It seems impossible!"

PROBABLY the whole thing seemed impossible to a farmer and his gangling son. They could not see Doc Savage's car. They were ludicrous figures in the invisible infra-red beam.

"Gosh whang your hides!" squawked the bearded farmer, raising a double-barreled shotgun. "I'll learn you skunks to come milkin' my Jerseys!"

Whoom! Whoom!

The shotgun belched again. The shot spattered with a *swish* into a weird scene. A score or more of nearly naked shadows were dancing. As the stinging shot plastered their hides, they howled. Their wild dance became wilder.

"*Ifehe! Ifehe! Ifehe!*" squawled several voices.

"Masai!" barked Count Cardoti. "That word means to run!"

Doc had the infra-red beam playing directly upon the contorted figures of the leaping savages. They looked like sharply-cut shadows. Ostrich plumes waved from shaved heads.

Loops of the Africans' ears drooped to their shoulders. These now were filled with curious objects. Some displayed shining cans that had contained food. The cans had been stripped of paper. Other ear loops held mirrors.

"Blast their hides, Willy!" yelled the farmer.

The gangling young fellow whanged with another gun. The dance became a rout. The savages started throwing short spears as they ran. The farmer and his son escaped being hit.

"Strange they should miss at that close range," said Count Cardoti. "The Masai are expert spearmen."

"You forget they are in total darkness," advised Doc. "The farmer and his son are shooting blindly. They cannot see the invisible beam with which we are observing them."

Realizing it was being fought in total darkness, the battle between the farmers and the Africans became ridiculous. The Masai squawked with pain and ran.

The shotguns whoomed in the direction of the yells. No doubt these weapons were loaded with fine birdshot. They did no great damage.

A number of spears stuck in the ground. They were tufted with ostrich feathers. These did not look red in the invisible beam.

THE FARMER produced a flashlight and cast its illumination around. Then he let out a loud oath.

"The danged, gosh-whanged skunks!" he bawled. "Damn if they ain't killed two of my best heifers!"

"We will keep out of this," advised Doc quietly. "We have other business."

Doc switched off the infra-red beam. He flicked the boring

headlights across the field. The old farmer jumped up and aimed his shotgun at the car.

"So that's where the wallopers come from!" he shouted. "Well, I'll pulverize yuh!"

Whoom! Whoom!

The shotgun belched straight at the sedan. Count Cardoti ducked his head. Birdshot pattered like rain on Doc's car. The man of bronze only smiled.

The sedan was impervious to even steel-jacketed slugs. The fine shot had no more effect than a handful of sand.

"We are friends," stated Doc quietly. "We heard the shooting."

The old man quit shooting. Doc and the others got out and climbed the fence into the field.

"I don't know who you are," said the older farmer suspiciously. "You ain't much whiter'n them dang skunks!"

The farmer's flashlight had picked out Doc's bronze face. Doc smiled slightly.

"You seem to have strange visitors here in the backwoods," he said. "Is this the first time?"

"It's the second time, an' the other time they killed one of my best heifers!" complained the farmer. "Lookit this!"

"Omophagous Ulotrichans," stated Johnny. "Well, I'll be superamalgamated, Doc!"

"What's that? Whatcha callin' me?" rapped the farmer.

"He means your visitors are eaters of raw flesh and drinkers of blood," stated Doc.

"Well, why in time don't he say so?" growled the farmer. "Lookit them heifers!"

"It would seem a ghastly rite has been performed," said the man of bronze. "Your visitors were following a native custom."

Two fine, yellow-hided Jersey cows lay on the ground. They were young heifers of the best stock. Around these two animals the Masai had been performing a tribal rite.

Doc Savage knelt beside each of the animals. His quick hands stripped away coils of brass wire. These had been wound tightly around the throats of the heifers.

Above each binding of wire appeared the wounds made by short arrows. The big veins of the Jerseys had been tapped.

Though they were now in a land where salt might be had in abundance, these blood-drinking savages had reverted to a custom of their tribal land. In that land there was no salt. The natives obtained it from living blood.

"They keep some animals alive and use them for this purpose," explained Doc Savage. "Now we will see what a bit of magic will accomplish."

No doubt the old farmer thought it was magic. He did not observe Doc's hands closely enough. Doc had administered the contents of a hypodermic syringe. It had been injected into the veins of the prize Jerseys.

"Well, I'll be teetotally hornswoggled!" gasped the farmer.

Both Jerseys had come to life. The heifers scrambled awkwardly to their feet and bawled.

"Is there a William Smith living on Crooked Neck Road?" asked Doc.

"Never heard of no such feller hereabouts," said the farmer.

As they returned to the sedan, Johnny said, "That fixes the country these Africans come from. The blood-drinkers are in the region near Lake Jipe north of the Parri Mountains in Central East Africa."

"Renny is somewhere in the Parri Mountains," said Doc.

"He is among pleasant people," said Johnny.

"It looks bad for him," said Count Cardoti soberly. "They have a habit of inflicting the Long Juju torture on prisoners."

"Renny's big enough to take care of himself," declared Johnny.

"He is in bad country indeed," asserted Count Cardoti. "Besides these Masai and the Waperri, there are many fierce tribes, including the Warusha, Wataita, Watatura and Swahili. Then recently the Juju tribes of the Okoyongs and the Enyongs have come into the land."

"And they send a prince to Oxford for the privilege of being king over that mess!" observed Johnny.

DOC SAVAGE fixed the location of what should have been 4404 Crooked Neck Road.

"It is as I suspected," stated Doc. "There is no human habitation in this section."

The return address given on the teakwood block was hardly one to be found in the postal guide.

Fallen slabs of stone that had once been white marked a grass-grown field behind a tumble-down stone fence. The address was an old private burial ground.

The man of bronze stood close to the broken stone fence. He had turned toward the car. Suddenly he halted. His keenly trained auditory sense had picked up a sound.

The weird graveyard was filled with mellow, fantastic trilling. Doc sprang lightly over the old fence. From a pocket, he produced a bottle of powder. Walking a half circle, he sprinkled some of this on the grass.

"The abode of the departed has had recent visitors," said Johnny.

Count Cardoti saw glowing streaks on the long grass. The bottle contained a fluorescent chemical powder. The tender blades of grass were still moving. They had been trampled only a short time before.

Doc led the way back among the sunken graves.

"Well, I'll be superamalgamated!" rapped Johnny. "Apparently they have been head-hunting as well as drinking blood."

Doc's generator flashlight widened its beam. The illumination revealed two human heads. They were the heads of Africans, with gruesomely distorted ears.

On each head was an old hat of straw.

But the heads had not been severed. They were attached to bodies. Two dead Masai had been buried in this queer fashion.

"It is a custom of the Masai to bury their dead sitting up," stated the erudite Johnny. "Later, they preserve the skulls and keep them around as family heirlooms."

"True," shuddered Count Cardoti. "And a jolly ghostly custom it is. I have seen the practice among the tribes of Kokoland."

The dead men had been given all of the tribal ceremony. The corpses had been stripped. The black skins glistened with an anointment of ground-nut oil. They had been marked with symbols.

Doc Savage seemed to have lost interest in the buried warriors. He had produced the square box with the lens of the black light. Walking slowly in a circle, he moved to a position back of the two bodies.

Count Cardoti suddenly saw queerly glowing spots. There were two sets of these. They were about as far apart as men's heels would have touched.

Johnny saw what Doc was doing.

"Well, I'll be superamalgamated!" he exclaimed. "Nobody but Ham and Monk could have left those prints!"

Doc's men wore heels of spongy rubber. They contained a chemical which left this definite fluorescent trace.

The trail of Ham and Monk lay through the sunken graveyard.

Chapter VI

TWO LIVING HEADS

THE heads of the dead Waperri were not the only heads on the ground tonight in the Long Island wilderness. There were two other heads. The heads of the dead men were gruesome.

The other two heads would have been ghastly, if they hadn't been funny. At the same time, they were weird objects. For these two heads moved with nothing visible to cause the motion.

The skulls had hair and the faces of men. There in the blackness of that isolated, abandoned graveyard, the heads abused each other.

"There ain't a bit of doubt but what them heathen mistook you for one of their close relatives!" rasped a strident voice. "And I suppose they put me out here so you'd have company!"

The other head let out a chuckling squawk.

"Yeah?" it stated in a high-pitched voice. "Seeing you're so full of conversation, I'd like to see you talk yourself outta this mess! If I only had Habeas Corpus here, he'd dig me out!"

"I'd rather stay where I am than have that shote kicking dirt in my face," said the first head. "What do you suppose those devils did with Pat?"

"Howlin' calamities!" groaned the other head. "I've been tryin' not to think about that! Ouch! There's a danged ant bitin' my ear!"

Having an ant working on an ear when your head hasn't any visible body is annoying. Monk's ears were fairly well protected by his furry, stiff red hair, but Long Island raises some big, black ants with forcible pincers. Monk howled.

"Confound you, insects!" rasped the adjoining head. "Stop that squawking or your cousins might come back! If they do, they'll probably make a good job by shaving you off close to the ground!"

"Yeah?" howled Monk. "An' if they done the same thing to you, they wouldn't have nothin' an' they wouldn't leave nothin'."

"Shut up!" rapped the usually sartorially elegant Ham. "Hear that? Somebody's shooting!"

This man at the moment the irate farmer was engaged in chasing a few, assorted wild African warriors out of his cow pasture.

THE distant guns whoomed faintly. Then everything became still.

"Thunderation!" rapped out Ham's head suddenly. "Now the mosquitoes have found us!"

Monk's head must have grinned in the darkness.

"Keep on talkin'," said his head, "an' maybe the hot air'll burn 'em up the way it does your friends."

The shotguns whanged again in the distance. In one of the near-by trees, a lonesome owl hooted. Ham and Monk shivered.

"I'll betcha that danged Señorita Moncarid had something to do with this," complained Monk. "There was some kind of a fight downstairs in the warehouse before they hauled us out."

"Pat isn't so sure where the señorita stands," replied Ham. "She knows there are two gangs of these Africans. One gang looks as if the señorita belongs to it. They have arched noses and are lighter in color than the others. The gangs could be mixed up in a fight over Señorita Moncarid herself."

"Dag-gonnit?" squeaked Monk. "Who is she, anyway? I guess the señorita's gang took Pat away. I think then they run into this other crowd with the funny ears, and the funny ears licked 'em. Anyway, we're here, what little is stickin' above ground."

"In your case, it's only your head an' that ain't much," cut in Ham's head. "Now take me, the best part of me is still outside."

"I only hope a squirrel comes along and jumps down your shyster throat!" exploded Monk. "What do you suppose all that dancin' was about?"

THE dance had been a fantastic orgy. When they had buried Ham and Monk, the loop-eared warriors had stripped off most of their American clothes. Their remaining garments had been Colobus monkey fur.

To the rhythm of a weird chanting, the Masai had formed a circle around the protruding heads. All had brandished long spears. Their shaved heads had been adorned with red ostrich feathers.

Along with Ham and Monk, the Masai had brought along two warriors who had been killed in the clash at the warehouse.

The burial of Ham and Monk alive with only their heads exposed, likely was the Masai's idea of carrying out a tribal rite. In addition to burying their warriors sitting up, with the heads outside, the Masai make a practice of sending along some living relative to keep a dead man company.

Perhaps they imagined Ham and Monk would serve in the absence of the nearest of kin.

Now Ham and Monk saw an approaching light. A car stopped near the highway side of the old burial ground.

Voices murmured beyond the trees. A little later, the pencil ray of a flashlight flicked over the ground.

"Well, I'll be double-and-triple-superamalgamated!" exploded the voice of Johnny. "I've always expected to witness this phenomenon! Ham and Monk have fought each other right down to terra firma at last!"

"Of all the incredible happenings!" exclaimed Count Cardoti. "They've buried these men alive!"

Doc Savage played the flashlight over the moving heads.

"They do seem to be living," he stated solemnly.

"Perhaps we have fallen under the spell of their Long Juju and this demonstration is only an hallucination hypnotically induced," stated Johnny.

"Howlin' calamities, Doc!" squeaked Monk. "A dag-goned ant's eatin' one of my ears! Get me outta here!" Then he suggested cheerfully, "You might leave that shyster, so's them heathen won't be disappointed when they come back!"

"Wait'll I get out of here!" promised Ham. "I'm going to slice off both of your baboon ears!"

Count Cardoti stared at the bickering heads. Doc and Johnny made the dirt fly. "We've got to get on the trail of Pat," declared Ham. "I believe the gang with Señorita Moncarid took her."

"I wonder how much this señorita might be mixed up in the murder of my poor friend?" said Count Cardoti.

"Perhaps when we have found Pat, my cousin, we may have an answer," stated Doc. "There seems no more we can discover here. This William Smith, who sent the teakwood block, selected a strange address."

Doc Savage was speculating at the moment if the sender of that mysterious package could have had a purpose in the return address. Undoubtedly the sender of the teakwood block must have known the old burial ground had been made a location for primitive savage ceremonies.

Doc Savage and his men returned to headquarters. Their immediate purpose was to rescue Patricia Savage.

This remarkable and beautiful young woman needed no rescuing. She was seated calmly in Doc's library.

"I was about to start out looking for you," stated Pat. "I thought we would try and save Ham and Monk. It seems that chore has been accomplished."

"We found them buried to their necks in an old graveyard," said Johnny solemnly.

Pat smiled sweetly upon the pair.

"It should keep them cool for a while," she suggested. "Doc, I have something I must show you."

The man of bronze accompanied her into the laboratory.

"This Señorita Moncarid who got me into this jam, Doc," she said, "it seems she also got me out of it. I have discovered there are two battling factions of Africans in New York."

"That is pretty generally suspected by this time," said Doc dryly. "Any more news?"

"Yes," snapped Pat. "Plenty. Renny is in trouble, isn't he? Well, this señorita is somehow mixed up with one of the African gangs. They are Kokonese, and with them they have some Wataveta warriors. Señorita Moncarid has represented herself as Spanish. After I was set free, I didn't see her. But one of the Kokonese handed me this message.

The message was from Señorita Moncarid:

FORGIVE MY DECEPTION. I REALLY CAME FROM SPAIN. A SPANISH FAMILY, FRIENDLY WITH MASAI TRIBESMEN, SENT ME HERE TO BE EDUCATED. YOUR LIFE IS ENDANGERED. I HAVE BEEN TOLD TO GET IN TOUCH WITH DOC SAVAGE. I DO NOT KNOW WHAT ALL THIS MEANS. I HEAR THE KOKONESE SAY SOMETHING ABOUT KEEPING A BLOOD IDOL FROM THE MASAI—SEÑORITA MONCARID.

Returning with Pat to the outer room, Doc said, "Pat, you will go home now. I wish you to forget all of this. The señorita has spoken the truth. I do not want you to be involved in the danger which threatens."

Pat looked at her bronze cousin with a little smile.

"I was sure that was the way it would be," she said. "But I'll bet something happens to let me get in on this one."

"Not if you remain at home where you belong," stated Doc.

Count Cardoti was a polished young man. There was no doubt of the approval with which he regarded Doc's beautiful cousin.

Pat seemed to find Count Cardoti appealing. The title before his name had nothing to do with this. Count Cardoti had an Oxford finish.

"I think you have been befriended by some of the most loyal subjects of King Udu, Miss Savage," said the count. "The whole land over there has come under the curse of the Long Juju brought in by wandering Okoyong from the South African coast."

"I would be delighted to study this witchcraft at close range," commented Pat, with one eye on Doc.

"It is not so romantic when seen at close range," advised Count Cardoti. "In the end, I suppose only the conquest and domination of the white race can settle the tribal differences."

"I believe I'm going to visit your country," stated Pat, still with the idea of effect upon Doc Savage.

But Doc Savage was no longer present. He had vanished silently.

THE man of bronze whipped from his special elevator into his underground garage. From here he passed through a paneled door. Doc had chosen a strange route.

He was now in one of the subway tunnels. A downtown train roared its thunderous warning. Doc stepped aside into one of the lighted niches. When the train had passed, Doc glided toward the nearest exit.

A few minutes later, he was again ascending toward his headquarters. But he was using an entrance which emerged from the wall of the laboratory.

The man of bronze was in the laboratory only a few seconds. He departed by the same route he had come. The voices of his companions had been murmuring in the library.

When Doc Savage again had appeared before the others, Ham and Monk were glaring balefully at Count Cardoti. Pat Savage was preparing to depart. Count Cardoti had offered to escort her home.

Pat had accepted with alacrity. Ham and Monk were burning up.

"If I can make contact with some of these Kokonese," Count Cardoti was saying, "perhaps I can get a clue to this mysterious Blood Idol. I would like, indeed, to clear it up. It might explain the assassination of Prince Zaban."

"Isn't it customary for the burial of a tribal prince to be carried out in his own land?" questioned Doc.

"Yes, it is a custom," said Count Cardoti. "But in this case I am afraid it will be impossible. I have cabled, but the message may be some time reaching King Udu. Arrangements have been made for a funeral here to-morrow. The body will be placed in a vault."

Doc Savage said nothing. His flaky gold eyes had taken in Johnny. The scholarly skeleton of a man casually moved from the room. He went into the laboratory.

PAT SAVAGE was just preparing to leave with Count Cardoti, when Johnny came rushing in.

"Doc! They've got it!" he shouted excitedly. "They've busted the safe with a torch an' grabbed the teakwood block!"

Johnny had to be greatly upset to state a fact so simply.

Count Cardoti followed the others as they whipped into the laboratory.

"By all the holies!" he cried. "That safe didn't look like it could be cracked!"

"It would have resisted most experts," stated Doc.

But the safe undoubtedly had been cracked. It appeared as if an electrical torch had been hooked into the wall. The connecting cord was still in evidence.

"Howlin' calamities!" whipped out Monk. "They made some job of it!"

The hard steel door hung by one of its ponderous hinges. The heavy tumblers of the lock had been sheered off as if by acid.

"The teakwood block!" exclaimed Count Cardoti.

Doc Savage said nothing. The exposed interior of the safe was the answer. Where the block had reposed, the shelf of the safe had been crumpled. The secret exit behind the tropical fish tank was partly open.

"Oh, I'm glad it happened!" declared Pat Savage.

Doc Savage was running his fingers along the seared edges of the steel.

"I agree with you, Miss Savage," stated Count Cardoti. "I am very much afraid there might have been death in that wooden block."

"It might be there is death in it," stated Doc. "If so, it is most important that we discover it."

Chapter VII

SHRINE OF LONG JUJU

IT was not yet midnight in Manhattan when Patricia Savage departed from Doc's headquarters. She was accompanied by Count Cardoti. Nothing had been discovered to afford a trace to the thief who had taken the teakwood block.

Doc Savage and his companions were left with the wrecked safe.

The man of bronze seemed to lose interest in the robbery.

As soon as Pat and Count Cardoti had departed, Doc stepped to a wall panel in the laboratory. His hand moved a switch.

"Well, it sure looked like a real job," grinned Monk. "Anyway, that count guy won't be worrying about the block blowing up."

As Doc pushed the switch, the whole wrecked safe moved. It slid to one side and disappeared where there apparently had been blank wall. Immediately behind it stood Doc's big safe. It had not been touched.

The cracked front and the sagging door were false.

"I feared Count Cardoti might concern himself needlessly," was all the explanation the man of bronze offered. "Now we must see if Renny's transmitter can be picked up."

A FEW thousand miles away, the chances for communicating with Renny seemed slim. Though it was at the midnight hour in New York, there was the hint of dawn coming in the far-away Parri Mountains.

At the edge of a dripping jungle, six persons were chained to the smooth trunks of *senecio* trees.

Renny had been given an extra load of the chains. These were of the manacle type used on slaves. They were thick with the corroding red rust of the tropics. Many pounds were on Renny's limbs.

But in the rust and roughness was weakness. Slowly, with infinite caution, Renny was setting his strength against the shackles. He had to be careful to prevent the *senecio* tree bending.

First of Renny's fellow prisoners was Souho. The huge hunter had the failing of his race. Superstition filled him with fear. This turned his blood to water. The slow chanting and the *tunk-tunk-tunk* of the log-skin drums were more terrible to Souho than the fangs and claws of the fiercest beasts.

Mapanda, the Arabian half-caste, came next. He was not afraid. His midnight eyes were like polished black beads. He was fiercely loyal to Renny.

Two miserable natives, evidently captured enemies, sat in their chains. Like all of their kind, they were resigned to death. Their eyeballs were rolled until only the whites showed.

The sixth prisoner was an aged black woman. She was not held by chains. They were unnecessary.

All of the prisoners understood they were to die. With four

it was fate. The coming of dawn over the blue lake with its snow-white cranes near-by would be the signal.

Renny was no fatalist. The big engineer didn't believe he was going to die. The hideous, leering faces of the bedaubed warriors did not inspire him with terror.

They only made Renny mad. He had a railroad to build. It would link an Indian Ocean seaport with an inner native kingdom.

Water chugged in the blue lake. Heads with protruding knobs were sticking up. These were hippopotamuses. White cranes flew about them. The river flowed into the lake. Its water was slow, sluggish.

Over all this the light of the sun came with the suddenness of an explosion.

Tunk-tunk-tunk banged the monotonous skin drums.

"THUNDERATION!" growled Renny to Mapanda. "Why don't the fool heathen stop jumpin' around and get down to cases?"

Twoscore oddly painted warriors continued their slow circling. They swung long spears in circles, within inches of the prisoners' noses.

Renny set one tremendous arm against the weakest links of the tropically rusted chains. He heard a metallic snap.

Back of the prancing warriors stood the grotesque figure of the man in a lion's pelt. The head of the beast topped his face. The fangs and claws dangled about his ears. Renny knew he was a white man.

He was "The Shimba." He was giving the orders.

In the middle of the slow, little river was a small island.

Upon this island reared a square shrine of polished woods. On this burned the fire of a cooking pot. Old women stirred bubbling goats' meat, beans and blood in the big vessel.

The women moaned and chanted. They stirred the boiling mess with their bared, skinny hands.

On the square shrine weaved a fearsome figure. Renny knew this was a priest of the Long Juju. He was known as a *Papa Loi*. At the corner sat a huddled priestess garbed in red ostrich feathers. She was the *Maman Loi*.

The *Papa Loi* was wrapped in a red robe of store calico. His fantastic head was intended to represent a skull. It was a crude mask.

The slow water flowed around the little island toward the blue lake with the white cranes.

With the daylight, the fire around which the warriors had been dancing, became only a smudge of smoke.

"Holy cow!" boomed Renny. "Hey, funny face! When do we come to something?"

"It would be well to make to talk with wisdom, *b'wana*," murmured Mapanda. "They make do ready for the appearing of Long Juju!"

Tunk-tunk-tunk!

The warriors suddenly ceased prancing. They set their long spears in the ground.

The Shimba strode into the circle with a grand gesture. Renny was not impressed.

"Cut out the clowning, funny face!" he rumbled. "Say what's on your mind, an' get it over with!"

"*B'wana* Renwick has little wisdom," spoke The Shimba impressively in English. "The *Inglesi* never will build their railroad. This King Udu on whom you depend, is old, and fat, and foolish. He is soon to die. He has refused the faith of the Long Juju."

"Long Juju, my eye!" exploded Renny. "You're not scarin' me with all this tommyrot! You'd better call off this bunk or there'll be a guy worse than a thousand King Udus right on your tail!"

"Foolish talk will accomplish nothing," droned the voice of The Shimba. "You must give up this railroad. You will be conducted with your *safari* back to Muoa Pemba. That is the last word of The Shimba."

"Bunk!" roared Renny. "Wait till Doc Savage—"

The Shimba interrupted with an angry snarl.

"The cheap magic of the bronze man will avail nothing against the power of the Long Juju!" he shouted. "*B'wana* Renwick must be shown!"

The white man with his flapping lion's pelt whirled upon the Masai warriors. He barked an order in their own tongue.

"*B'wana* Renwick, they make do for test of Long Juju death," said Mapanda huskily. "They who make not believe die in red water."

RENNY was straining fiercely at other links of his rusted chains. The big engineer was sure he could break loose if he had the time. Already, he was estimating where he would start mowing down Masai with his ponderous fists.

At The Shimba's order, the two chained warrior prisoners

and the unfettered old woman were seized by the Masai. The Long Juju priest fluttered his bony fingers from the island of the shrine. He gestured, as if inviting the three cringing natives to join him on the island.

There was no movement on the surface of the slow, little river. Renny could see the water was shallow. It looked as if any person could easily wade out to the island of the Long Juju.

"*Ai-ee! Ai-ee! Ai-ee!*"

It was the old woman moaning. She was being pushed toward the low bank of the river. The chains of the other two native prisoners were dropping from their arms and legs.

"*Ai-ee!*" they took up the moaning chant. "*Ai-ee! Ai-ee!*"

"Holy cow!" boomed Renny. "What the devil an' all are they scared about?"

"They must walk to the altar of the Long Juju, *B'wana* Renwick," said Mapanda. "If they come do through water, the Long Juju is make do pleased, and they will live."

"Well, what are they groanin' about?" growled Renny. "There ain't any crocs in sight an' the water ain't deep!"

The long hands of the *Papa Loi* fluttered toward the shore.

"*Ai-ee-ai-ee!*" screamed the old native woman.

She was the first to go into the water. At the points of Masai spears the captive men also were forced in the river to their waists.

All three prisoners were screaming now. This did not make sense to Renny. It looked as if a couple of jumps would put any able-bodied person on that island. Even the old woman ought to be able to wade the shallow river.

The Masai warriors hopped up and down along the shore. Their red ostrich feathers quivered in the breeze.

The two black men and the old woman were halfway from the shore to the Long Juju island. The water was only a little above their waists.

Renny did not see any movement in the sluggish river. So it could not have been a crocodile. A crocodile would have heaved his body to the surface.

"Thunderation!" gulped the big engineer. "Look at 'em!"

Souho, the black hunter, moaned and rocked his massive, kinky head with his chin sunk on his breast.

Mapanda hissed through his white teeth.

Scream after scream squawled from the throat of the two

men in the river. The old woman did not scream. Her frail shrunken arms suddenly were thrust upward and her feeble body went under the quiet surface.

"HOLY COW!" rasped Renny. "What is it?"

"The Long Juju, they say, *b'wana,*" muttered Mapanda. "The Long Juju is not pleased."

The two natives leaped in the water. They slapped down with their hands. Over them waved the skinny arms of the *Papa Loi.* The Long Juju priest was chanting in frenzied exultation.

Slap-slap-slap, went the hands of the natives in the river.

Then they must have sunk to their knees. Still, no body of any attacking crocodile appeared. Around the spot where the old woman had vanished, and where the natives were going down, the water was turning to scarlet.

"*Ai-ee—ai-ee!*" screamed the last of the prisoners.

Already the other had become only a few bubbles showing on the red water. Now the third one went. And on his face Renny saw such a look of agony and horror as he had never before witnessed.

Then the slow, little river was still. Its red surface had ceased churning. It flowed tranquilly toward the blue lake with the white cranes flying.

"It's crazy!" rumbled Renny. "There ain't anything in there!"

The Masai were prancing madly. They shook their hideous faces over the edge of the river. Suddenly The Shimba rapped out a command.

Before Renny realized what the next movement would be, two huge warriors had seized upon Mapanda. They pulled him loose from his chains.

"*B'wana* Renwick!" moaned the loyal, half-caste youth.

"Keep your hands off him!" shouted Renny. "Whatever it is, if you put him in there, I'll tear you to pieces one at a time!"

The Shimba mocked him with a sneering tone.

"*B'wana* Renick will perhaps give up this crazy railroad then?"

"No! Not in a million years!" yelled Renny. "You wouldn't dare—"

Beside him, Souho, the native hunter, was moaning over

and over again, "They feed Long Juju—they feed Long Juju—"

"Very well then!" rapped the voice of The Shimba.

No doubt but Renny would have changed his position if he had been given the chance. He might even have abandoned the railroad plan, temporarily, to have saved Mapanda. But the Masai were now lusting for the sight of more blood.

Some of the chains clanked on Mapanda's slender arms. The African boy's hands were uplifted as he was plunged into the river. But the youth did not cry out again.

Renny heaved against the multitude of rusted chains binding him to the *senecio* tree. The Shimba laughed mockingly, tauntingly.

"*B'wana* Renwick, the great Renny, will see the power of the Long Juju!"

The *Papa Loi* chanted. Mapanda was in the river to his waist. Whatever it was had snatched the three prisoners, its voracious hunger must have been aroused.

Mapanda was only waist deep, a few feet from the shore. Masai spears still pushed cruelly into his bared flesh. Across the African boy's face came a spasm of pain.

But Mapanda was stoical. He did not cry out. Only his eyes looked mournfully at Renny. Then he was sinking, going down in the water.

Around Mapanda boiled a reddening pool. Yet no fangs or head had appeared.

Mapanda was looking at Renny. His lips were moving. It seemed as if the part of his body under the water was being dissolved into scarlet flesh.

AT the base of the smooth *senecio* tree, an earthquake erupted. No bull gorilla ever roared more mightily. The sturdy tree was almost uprooted. Renny had unleashed a maddened strength.

The rusted, weakened links of the many chains started snapping. Mapanda's head and shoulders were still above water. The *Papa Loi* was crying out his chant with unholy delight. The ancient women with the boiled arms ceased stirring the devilish mixture in the bubbling pot.

Before The Shimba could issue a command, or his Masai warriors could swing their spears, the giant Renny became a hurtling mass of enraged flying chains and bone. His massive fists, with deadly links enwrapping his wrists, swung with the force of trip hammers.

Two Masai warriors yelled and went ahead of the big engineer into the river. They had been hit so hard their bodies turned over twice before they splashed into the bloody water.

Renny reached Mapanda with one jump from the shore. He pulled Mapanda into his big arms.

Mapanda's eyes were closing. He opened them slowly.

"Thanks, too much, *B'wana* Renwick," he whispered weakly.

All of the boy's body became like a rag. Renny knew he was dead. The blood had been drained from his veins.

The big engineer started wading back toward the shore. A hundred stabbing pains shot through his legs. Perhaps only the leathers to his knees and the rough cords of his trousers saved him. But even these could not altogether resist a thousand needlelike teeth that sunk into his flesh.

Renny saw the flash in the bloody water. So this was the Long Juju. There were millions of tiny, flesh-eating fish. They were only three or four inches long.

Despite their miniature size, these tropical man-eaters are the worst killers of jungle waters.

WITH Mapanda in his arms, Renny reached the muddy shore. The big engineer saw scores of the vicious fish clinging to his legs.

Renny roared again. The pain in his legs meant nothing. For a moment the shocked Masai warriors had stood motionless. Where the two had been knocked into the river, now were reddening pools.

"Get him!" yelled The Shimba. "Run the *Inglesi* through!"

At the command, half a dozen warriors attempted to obey. They charged with their long spears held stiffly.

"You killin' devils!" boomed Renny.

The spear points were jamming toward him. The Masai's eyes were red rimmed. Renny wished greatly for the bullet-proof garments of fine chain mesh which Doc Savage had devised for his men. But the engineer was not wearing these. He knew grimly he had only one chance.

One small object reposed in the little watch pocket at the top of his cord trousers. It was something he had planned to test on one of the isolated mountain walls.

A spear blade grazed Renny's head. He could do only what he did. He had made every effort to save Mapanda. The youth had died. Now Renny lifted the body in his huge hands and drove directly upon the spears of the Masai.

He knocked down half a dozen warriors with the bleeding body. Dropping the corpse, Renny caught up a fallen spear. He did not make the mistake of using its blade.

The heavy haft of the long spear mowed a circle around the roaring giant. Masai skulls cracked. One warrior's neck was broken. The Shimba was dancing excitedly, urging the spearmen to the kill.

Renny stumbled over an object on the ground. A spear blade clipped a chunk from his shoulder. Renny arose with a great shield of dried oxhide.

Directly before him were a dozen rallying warriors. They must have had the same sensation as if an army had charged upon them. The shield and the spear became terrible weapons with Renny's bull-like muscles behind them.

Renny had cleared a space all around him. But there were too many Masai. They were moving warily now.

"Come on an' fight, you killers!" bellowed the enraged engineer.

Under cover of the shield, he dropped the spear. He thumbed a small round object from the watch pocket of his cords. This was no larger than a child's play marble. On its side was a tiny lever.

Chapter VIII

WHEN THE BOX OPENED

RENNY estimated the position of his surrounding enemies. They were between him and the island of the Long Juju.

The engineer stooped low. Spears thudded upon the great oxhide shield. One point pierced the hide into Renny's arm.

Renny's right hand flipped upward. His thumb nail had

flicked the lever on the small globe. The object became a mere flash of light flying through the air.

Renny hurled himself backward. He saw The Shimba running madly into the jungle. The Shimba was a smarter man than his warriors. The more stupid Masai were charging.

Renny flung himself beside Souho, the native hunter. The big oxhide shield covered their bodies.

The air itself seemed to explode. The hurtling object had not reached the island of the Long Juju shrine. It had burst in mid-air. It was a diminutive grenade containing what was perhaps the world's highest-powered explosive.

The shrine of the Long Juju, with the *Papa Loi*, the old women beside the boiling pot, and the island itself seemed to dissolve.

The slow, little river heaved from its shallow bed. For scores of yards, it became transformed into flying rain. With the water, came a deluge of millions of tiny, voracious fish.

The diminutive man-eaters lay gasping, snapping their needlelike teeth.

Such of the Masai warriors as were not blown from their feet and brained against the trees, were trying to crawl away.

The Shimba had disappeared.

Renny wrenched loose the chains of the moaning Souho.

Souho stared unbelievingly at the place where the island of the Long Juju had been.

"No make do believe, *B'wana* Renwick," he mumbled.

The giant hunter knelt at Renny's feet, clinging to his hands.

"Holy cow!" boomed the engineer. "Get up, you fool! I oughta used that on 'em last night! It would have saved poor Mapanda!"

Renny led the way back toward their camp. Not a breath stirred in the jungle.

"We've got to dig up the radio transmitter an' get word to Doc," announced Renny.

AT this time, Doc Savage, back in Manhattan, was trying to pick up a possible short wave signal from Renny. The signal came. It was indistinct at first.

A few thousand miles away, Renny was sweating to keep that generator going. The transmitter had not been demolished. A Masai had made the attempt with a spear. Renny had repaired the damage.

Ham, Monk and Johnny were crowded around the man of bronze. They were delighted to hear Renny.

"I'm free—lost all but one—King Udu needs help—"

Renny was saving all the words he could. His generator sputtered. The short wave squawked with the screaming interference of some ship at sea. Renny's voice came on again.

"King Udu is dying—his son must take throne—The Shimba threatens with Long Juju—Northern Legion planning conquest—tribes follow Blood Idol—King Udu has sent—"

The interference broke in on the crippled transmitter. Doc Savage worked rapidly to pick up more. It came in spaced jerks.

"King Udu great ruler—family eight generations—must have Blood Idol—King Udu very ill—need you greatly, Doc —"

Doc Savage broke in with a message.

"Prince Zaban has been slain. Who is next ruler?"

Renny's reply came slowly, the words being jumbled.

"No other heir—Prince Zaban must be—must be buried in Kokoland—demand ceremony—tribal custom or family ceases to rule—"

Renny was trying to send a further message. But his generator went out. Doc Savage could only understand the evil Shimba was behind most of the trouble. Doc suspected there might be a great treasure in the Kilimanjaro Mountains.

"We have no time to waste," Doc stated. "Renny is temporarily free. But he has lost his *safari*. The danger for him is very great."

THE man of bronze was opening the big safe. From it, he removed the polished teakwood block. The closest scrutiny had not revealed so much as a seam or crack.

Doc Savage amazed his companions. He had become unusually cautious with the teakwood block. Now he used the radio beam which operated the electroscopic lock of the door leading into the library.

Perhaps the teakwood block lay in the path of the beam. Monk let out a shrill exclamation.

"Howlin' calamities! Lookit, Doc!"

The man of bronze was taking no chances. He whipped over to the table. The upper half of the teakwood block must have been fitted by a cabinetmaker more skillful than most. Where there had not been the faintest hair line of division in the wood, was now a gap that slowly opened wider.

"Stay back," cautioned Doc. "There still may be danger."

But if he believed there was peril, the bronze giant ignored it for himself. He lifted the heavy teakwood in his hands. All of the upper half had slid open. Doc's flaky gold eyes gazed at the inside of the mysterious box.

He spoke no words. His fantastic trilling spoke for itself. The man of bronze had seen something amazing.

Monk, Johnny and Ham were standing close by. But before any of the three could look inside the box, Doc was slowly closing the lid.

"Brothers, this box contains a single jewel," he stated. "Only one, but I would judge it is beyond all price. I never suspected such a gem could exist. We must guard this with our lives."

The mystic box had again become what appeared to be a solid block of wood.

"We must prepare to join Renny at once, in Kokoland," advised Doc. "Count Cardoti will accompany us. He should be of the greatest assistance."

"I don't know whether I trust this Count Cardoti too far," said Ham.

"Yes," drawled Johnny. "He is now escorting Pat home."

PAT SAVAGE was at this time with Count Cardoti in a taxicab. The car was threading through thick traffic in Fifth Avenue. Count Cardoti was nervous.

"These taxi drivers keep me on edge," he said to Pat. "I'd rather risk some of the wildest beasts of the jungle."

Pat Savage laughed musically.

"Perhaps if I get to see Kokoland, I'll know more about it," she stated.

"Will Mr. Savage permit you to join this expedition?"

"Not if he can find some excuse to keep me at home," smiled Pat. "Doc seems to think I ought to be put in a glass case and kept for exhibition purposes."

"Well, I agree with that," said Count Cardoti gallantly. "But I would like it tremendously if you could accompany us."

"I might do it yet," mused Pat. "Lots of things can happen

in a very short time. I understand there will be a big funeral for your friend, Prince Zaban, this afternoon."

"Yes," said Count Cardoti heavily. "It is unfortunate, but I can see no way to return Prince Zaban to his native land."

Pat Savage did not seem to be listening. The taxicab was dodging other vehicles by inches. The driver slid under the nose of a double-deck bus.

Pat Savage was leaning forward. She was looking at the rear window of a big sedan. The sedan was moving rapidly away.

"Miss Savage! Look out, you'll be hurt!"

Count Cardoti exclaimed with apprehension, for Pat Savage had snapped open the door of the taxi. Her graceful figure was in the street. Another taxi and a small delivery truck bore down upon her.

"Miss Savage!" yelled Count Cardoti.

He had attempted to follow. The delivery truck blocked his way. Pat Savage dodged it by a few inches.

A traffic policeman whistled shrilly. Drivers hooted their horns.

"She'll be killed!" shouted Count Cardoti. "Can't you get to her, fellow?"

He was talking to his taxi driver. The driver scowled and let out an oath.

"Tryin' to beat it on me, huh?" he grunted. "Hey, you come across with the fare before you do any fadeout!"

Count Cardoti fumbled a bill from his pocket. He slapped it into the driver's hand. When he turned Pat Savage had disappeared somewhere in the midst of it.

Half a block away, Count Cardoti saw the door of a black sedan open and close.

IN the rear window of the sedan, Pat Savage had seen the lovely, dark face of Señorita Moncarid.

The driver of the sedan was an African. He had a thin, arching nose. He glanced swiftly at Pat Savage, then held the car until she had entered.

Pat noted this was the same chauffeur who had been knocked out in the attack at the East Side warehouse.

"Oh, it's you, Miss Savage!" exclaimed the señorita. "You must not be seen with me! It is very dangerous! I am going away and I had hoped you would not find me!"

"I had suspected that," stated Pat. "But I imagine we can find a number of things to discuss."

Señorita Moncarid protested. But the black sedan whirled away in traffic, carrying Doc's cousin.

SHORTLY after this time, Doc Savage's own sedan glided up to a shabby looking warehouse on the Hudson River. This building bore an inconspicuous sign, "HIDALGO TRADING COMPANY."

The name Hidalgo had little connection with the purpose of this warehouse. It was the designation of a town in Central America. Through that city, from the fabulous treasure of a surviving nation of Mayans, came the millions which supported Doc Savage's great purpose in righting wrongs and punishing evildoers.

But few would have guessed this weather-beaten warehouse was the home of the world's most modern air and undersea devices.

Streamlined planes were ready for departure to any of the four corners of the world at a few minutes' notice.

But the aircraft which Doc already had ordered prepared for the flight to Central East Africa was the strangest of all. It was neither a dirigible nor an airplane. It looked like a single, great wing.

As the man of bronze drove his sedan into the narrow street near the warehouse, he laid one hand suddenly on Johnny's wrist.

"Take the wheel," he said. "I shall rejoin you presently."

The sedan did not cease its forward motion. Doc had whipped from under the wheel. Johnny slid his long, bony body into the driver's seat. Doc was out of the car. He had vanished between two buildings.

"What was it?" inquired Ham. "I didn't see anything."

Neither had Doc's two other companions. Doc alone had caught the glimpse of the dark face in a small areaway. The man of bronze glided around the building. He came upon two Africans.

Neither could have heard the movement behind them. Both men were still watching the sedan intently. Johnny had just driven it into the doorway of the old warehouse. The door had closed.

Then one of the Africans suddenly whipped around. From his belt flashed a game-stabbing knife.

"*Ifehe! Ifehe!*" the man shouted.

He meant, "Run! Run!" His companion had only time to see a great, bronze giant hurtling upon him.

The man with the knife threw the weapon. The keen, heavy blade became a flash of light in the sun. Its point was directed at Doc's skull. The knife hurler was accurate. The blade struck and parted Doc's smooth bronze hair neatly.

There was a terrible, metallic *clank,* as if the heavy knife had split the bone of the bronze man's skull. The Africans, for the moment, must have been incapable of movement. Certainly they had expected to see the man of bronze topple to the pavement of the alley.

Doc's movement had not even been impeded. His bronze hands were faster than the eye could follow. Superstitious yells of fear burst from the throats of the Africans. They were cut off as if they had been garroted.

Doc's hands were on their throats. The thumbs found the great nerve centers at the tops of their spines. The eyes of the two men rolled until only the whites were visible. From under dirty turbans, the loops of their hideous ears slipped down and dangled. The two Africans seemed to go to sleep.

Doc seemed to lift off the whole top of his head. This was a close-fitting, bullet-proof metallic cap. Over it was hair exactly the same color as the bronze underneath.

Doc Savage disregarded one of the two men. The other he swung over his shoulder. He was inside the warehouse hangar within four minutes after he had left the car.

"Thunderation!" rasped Ham. "The devils are watching every move we make! Doc, it looks to me as if white brains were behind all this!"

"I haven't any doubt of it," stated Doc. "Oh, perhaps, educated brains which may be under a native thatch. We have not yet determined the part Señorita Moncarid is playing in all of this."

"What are you going to do with this fellow?" said Monk.

"He might be induced to speak," advised Doc. "We shall see when he recovers."

The bronze giant manipulated the nerve centers at the base of the brain. The African with the hideous ears slowly opened his smoky eyes. He acted as if he thought he had already died and entered the land of the Long Juju.

"You have been given orders by your *b'wana?*" stated

Doc, in native Masai. "He has talked with you not long ago?"

Doc's flaky gold eyes had a hypnotic quality. But they could not compel either fear or compliance in this black Masai. His own rolling orbs had no expression other than a touch of awe. He stared at Doc's smooth, bronze hair.

It was there he had seen his heavy knife strike. He thought he had heard the grinding of bone. Now there was not even a mark.

The Masai looked at Doc stupidly.

Doc Savage turned to direct the loading of his strange, new wing of the air.

"Watch this fellow closely, Monk," he directed. "After a while, he may be induced to tell us something."

In the street near the low warehouse, rubber squealed on the pavement. Count Cardoti climbed from a taxicab. He came running to the door of the warehouse.

As he came in, he said breathlessly, "They've got Miss Savage again! And Señorita Moncarid!"

"Howlin' calamities!" yelped Monk. "I know you wasn't to be trusted! Dag-gonit! What happened. I oughta take you apart!"

"You mean Pat was seized again by the men with Señorita Moncarid?" questioned Doc.

"Yes—well, no," said Count Cardoti. "Miss Savage seemed to go willingly. We were in a great tangle of traffic. Suddenly, she got out of the taxi and ran to a sedan. There was an African fellow driving. I'm sure I saw the dark face of a woman in the window of the sedan. Miss Savage got in. Before I could reach her, the car had been driven away."

"Sometimes Pat follows out her own ideas," said Doc. "But we shall have to investigate as soon as possible. Perhaps this Masai will be able to tell us something."

Count Cardoti had been looking at the prisoner. None had noticed the swift movement of one of the man's hands. His fingers had slipped to his mouth. Now his heavy jaws crunched something.

Doc Savage caught the Masai's wrist. The man only rolled his eyes. His head, with its hideous ears, lolled on one shoulder.

Doc Savage dropped the wrist.

"I should have taken greater care," he stated. "He must have been prepared for this. He would not speak."

The Masai never would speak. From his fingers dropped a small object of the size of a kidney bean.

Count Cardoti exclaimed, "The fellow took an *esere* bean! It's deadly! They use it among the natives to test the guilt or innocence of suspected murderers! And once they taste the *esere* bean, they never prove themselves innocent."

Doc Savage had vanished. He whipped into the alleyway, where the other man had been left senseless. The second Masai had disappeared.

Chapter IX

THREE BLACK HEARSES

PRINCE ZABAN's funeral was conducted the afternoon of the day following the self-poisoning of the Masai in Doc Savage's hangar. The cortege extended for several blocks. Manhattan always turns out for heroes living or royalty dead.

The usual crowd thronged before the exclusive funeral parlor. A line of police kept a space cleared. But while services were being conducted inside the chapel, into this clear space came a score of strange, solemn figures.

Manhattan has witnessed some strange rites. But never any more fantastic than this. The police, at first, would have blocked the Africans in their curious garb, or lack of it.

A wise, old police inspector issued an order. The score of strange mourners were permitted to proceed with what they had come to do.

They were tall, light-colored men. All had thin, arched noses. Their hair was twisted into fantastic knots. The powerful dark bodies glistened with ground-nut oil. Stripes of red-and-white ochre ornamented faces and breasts.

"*Ai-ee! Ai-ee! Ai-ee!*" chanted the Africans.

They formed in a solemn circle. They walked heel and toe, around and around. In the middle of the ring they deposited a curious object. This was an immense shield of oxhide. Around its edges were white ostrich feathers.

"*Ai-ee! Ai-ee! Ai-ee!*" droned the men.

One began thumping slowly with the heel of his hand, on dried skin stretched tight over a hollow piece of wood.

They kept on chanting. A gorgeous headdress was laid beside the oxhide shield. Some vessels containing cooked meat and beans were put with these. Around and around moved the circle of the impassive arched-nosed men.

"Dag-goned if I ever expected to see one of them voodoo heathen dances, right here in downtown Manhattan!" exclaimed Monk.

"It must make you feel very much at home," commented Ham.

With Johnny and Count Cardoti, Doc's companions had come from the funeral chapel. The assassinated Prince Zaban had been paid all the honor which Manhattan could give an African prince of the royal blood.

"Perhaps this ceremony may mean more than that in the chapel," said Count Cardoti. "It is the tribal rite of the Kokonese. I am surprised to know there are so many of Prince Zaban's own people in New York. It explains much of this trouble we have been having."

When the funeral cortege formed outside, the offerings of the chanting natives were placed in a separate motor car. This closely followed the black motor hearse at the head of the procession.

Doc Savage was not with his other men attending the funeral. At the time of the ceremony, the bronze giant had disappeared. He stated he had received a message from Patricia Savage.

Johnny and Ham walked slowly along the cars ready to move into the procession. They were disappointed. They had hoped to find Pat Savage and Señorita Moncarid.

Most of those in the procession were city notables. They were paying the civilized honors to the murdered man of royal blood. Ahead of the slowly moving motor hearse rode a dozen motor-cycle policemen.

"PERHAPS that tribal ceremony over here will have some effect on the kingdom of Kokoland," suggested Ham.

"I fear it would count for little," stated Count Cardoti. "Even if King Udu now had an heir, it is a tribal obligation that those of the ruling family shall be placed in the spot, which for eight generations, has been the burial crypt of the royal family. It is a tribal tradition that this must not be broken."

Owing to the ceremonial delays, the sun had gone down when the funeral cortege of Prince Zaban arrived in the vicinity of the cemetery.

As a tribute to Prince Zaban, a city official rode with the driver of the motor hearse. This driver was himself an African. His nose was thin and arched.

The sirens of the motor-cycle escort suddenly screamed. A lumbering truck had come into the avenue from a cross street. A traffic policeman was arguing with its driver. The driver had the hood lifted from the engine.

"After all that has happened, I don't like being held up until after dark," said the official beside the driver. "I wonder if we couldn't go around the block?"

The African driver spoke excellent English. Apparently he was an employee of the funeral establishment.

"We could go around this block," said the driver. "That truck may hold us up until long after it's dark."

A motor-cycle cop nodded, and headed up to the others of the escort. The procession halted for half a minute. The motor cycles swung into the side street. The truck ahead remained motionless.

In the narrow, darker side street, there was suddenly a mix-up among the motor-cycle men. Two automobiles had started across the head of the procession.

"Hey!" yelled a motor-cycle cop. "You ain't crossin' here!"

Others of the escort rode up to him. Then out of side alleys slid two more vehicles. The city official beside the hearse driver let out a gasp.

"Good grief!" he exclaimed. "There's something haywire about this! Look! There are two more motor hearses!"

A PAIR of big, black hearses rumbled into the narrow canyon of the street. Their drivers whirled them into the car tracks. One motor hearse skidded and almost collided with the other.

"*Hiya!*" shouted one of the motor-cycle cops. "Hold up there!"

But the fender of one hearse crashed into his machine. The

cop sprawled on the pavement. The other hearse ran down two of the motor-cycle men.

Africans were driving both hearses. One skidded to a stop directly in front of the motor hearse in the regular funeral cortege. Its rear door swung open. A stream of turbaned men poured into the street.

"Holy mackerel!" barked the official beside the arched-nosed driver. "Whoever heard of holding up a funeral?"

The motor-cycle men were now off their machines. A few carried clubs. These started smacking heads. Horns of the following autos created a bedlam of sound.

The city official continued squawking. He was struck over the head with a knobby club.

Other Africans were climbing onto the regular motor hearse. They attempted to seize the arched-nosed driver. One of his fists struck with unexpected speed. He knocked three men into the street.

Two men had reached the top of the motor hearse. One swung the heavy half of a short spear. The arched-nosed driver caught the blow across one ear. He slumped sideways. A turbaned man pushed him from the seat.

"Grab all them motor hearses!" shouted one of the motor-cycle cops. "Now I don't know which is which!"

Two small, closed cars seemed to lead two of the hearses out of the street. The motor-cycle cops were putting up a stiff fight. None had attempted to use a gun. It did not seem the thing to do in a mix-up over the funeral of a prince.

COUNT CARDOTI, with Ham, Monk and Johnny, hastened up.

"By all the holies!" he ejaculated. "What is all this unseemly disturbance! You would think a funeral procession would be respected!"

One of the motor-cycle cops with a blue knob over one eye came up. A motor hearse with the casket inside, was in place at the head of the procession. A tall, African driver sat on the seat.

"I don't know what it's all about," said the cop, "but the fellows jumped out of a couple of cars, then they beat it. I guess everything's all right."

"Everything's far from all right," rapped out Ham, the lawyer. "We've got the wrong hearse! And that's quite a lot all wrong!"

"You are undoubtedly correct," announced Count Cardoti.

"This is not our original funeral car. The body of Prince Zaban has been stolen!"

Newspaper and news reel photographers added to the jumble. They were getting spot news pictures. A prince of Africa had been assassinated, in the heart of the world's greatest city.

Now, apparently, the body of the prince had been stolen from the head of a funeral cortege.

"I wish Mr. Savage were here," declared Count Cardoti. "I cannot understand his absence. He intended to attend the funeral."

Doc had not appeared at the prince's funeral.

"I think Doc was interested in discovering the whereabouts of this Señorita Moncarid," stated Johnny. "He said we were to join him at the hangars on the Hudson. I believe he is having the *Wing* loaded to depart for Africa tonight."

"But good heavens!" insisted Count Cardoti. "I simply cannot leave New York until we recover the body of my poor friend!"

RAIN had begun to drizzle. This was an hour after the funeral abduction. On an unpaved road it made the mixed clay and sand slippery. A motor hearse rocked along this road.

The driver was one of the turbaned men. The vehicle came to an open space, where there had been a truck garden. A light winked and went out.

The motor hearse turned into the vacant field. Near the middle it was brought to a stop. The limp body of the arched-nosed driver was pushed to the ground.

The turbaned men gabbled in low voices. Two other cars stood at the edge of the field. Half a dozen men pulled the casket from its place. Many offerings and tokens of flowers had been heaped on the coffin.

The Africans set the casket on the ground. Several were for loading the coffin into one of the other cars, without further investigation. But the idea of one tall African prevailed. Hands unscrewed the lid.

Cries of rage and surprise went up. They crowded around the casket. Lights were brought.

The coffin was unoccupied. Apparently the motor hearse, which properly belonged at the head of Prince Zaban's funeral procession, had never contained a body. The superstition of the turbaned men with their hideously looped ear lobes cropped out.

A pair produced the short, stabbing spears. Uttering shouts of killing anger, they rushed upon the place where the driver of the arched nose had been tossed from the hearse. Again the night resounded with wild yells.

The driver had vanished. The mud showed where his body had lain. But tracks also indicated he must have recovered. He was no longer in the field.

"*Ifehe! Ifehe!*" yelled a voice.

Leaving the motor hearse in the middle of the field, the Africans fled. It was not until next day that the strange spectacle of the black hearse in an open field attracted attention.

The empty casket had been left as it had been opened. For the time, the police believed the body of Prince Zaban had been removed and taken away. The hearse driver with the arched nose was believed to have been murdered.

Chapter X

SOME STRANGE CRAFT

POLICE were baffled. The disappearance of Prince Zaban's corpse was added to New York's unsolved crime mysteries. Likewise, all traces to the whereabouts of the turbaned Africans were lost.

Nothing directed the search toward the Hudson River. The police would have been amazed, could they have seen the crew of a vessel having the lines of a speedy, ocean-going cruiser.

Aside from its lines of evident speed, the craft bore no distinguishing marks. Shortly after Prince Zaban's casket was found to be empty, there was great activity aboard this vessel.

Two other craft slipped out into the dark water from this

cruiser. They were long, low and narrow. Not enough of them was visible to mark them as different from anything that had ever been seen on the Hudson. It was the matter of their power which so marked them.

Thuck! Thuck! Thuck! Thuck!

Like the steady beat of drums. The thucking of wood on wood.

For each of these craft was propelled by twenty paddles. Ten were on each side. They rose and fell with the rhythm of clockwork.

Though they were man-driven, the long canoes moved with the speed of motor boats.

Besides the twenty paddlers to the canoe, there were ten other figures in each. These men were armed with long spears which stuck straight up into the darkness. A few occupants of the canoes carried short blowpipes. Some others carried bows and arrows. All of these weapons were adorned with ostrich feathers, dyed brightly red.

The canoes were like war craft. The kind of war craft which glide through the miasmatic mist of some jungle river in Africa, to attack a native village.

Only these primitive craft, with their old-fashioned weapons, were on their way to attack some of the most modern craft known to the world.

Thuck! Thuck! Thuck! Thuck!

They swept down toward the warehouse which housed Doc Savage's scientific air fleet. And at this moment, the most modern of all the aircraft was preparing to take off.

Doc Savage had reached the Hudson River hangar ahead of his companions and Count Cardoti. As he left his car, a great change took place in his appearance.

The man of bronze removed thin glass shells from his flaky eyeballs. These shells were like the smoky eyes of an African. He did something to his arched nose. Pieces of hard wax came loose in his hand.

When the deeper hue was cleaned from his bronzed skin, Doc was no longer the same man who had driven Prince Zaban's motor hearse in the funeral procession. He had stayed in the open field long enough to witness the terrified reaction of the turbaned Masai, when they had discovered the empty casket.

The man of bronze now wondered what would be the

result of their report to the brains commanding this expedition to New York. Would it be the distant Shimba, of whom Renny had reported, or would it be the nearer Señorita Moncarid who would get that report?

Doc Savage was convinced that at least both would eventually know of the ruse which had been employed to prevent the body of the prince being seized by his enemies.

Doc made no comment as Count Cardoti and his three companions arrived and told of the abduction of the motor hearse.

"We shall take off within the hour," Doc stated. "I believe we are sufficiently equipped to cope with some of the forces now menacing the land of the Kokonese."

Count Cardoti's bright, black eyes studied the strange, streamlined aircraft lying in one of the docks. He noted it seemed buoyant. It was like a giant wing without propellers.

Doc Savage's men had christened this new aircraft the *Wing*. It was neither airplane nor dirigible. But it was sustained by a new type of noncombustible gas of the greatest lifting capacity.

No propellers were visible on the smooth wing. Within the wing itself were tubes, or what might have appeared to be wind tunnels.

These tubes overcame the constant danger of propellers being snapped off at high speed.

"What is the motive force?" questioned Count Cardoti, as Doc's helpers were lashing many boxes aboard.

The erudite Johnny explained. Doc's newest ship was propelled by a new compound explosive of his own devising. This was composed of oil and air carried under high pressure into a forward combustion chamber.

Here the oil and air combined and burned with intense heat. The result, as in the cylinder of a Diesel engine, was to produce a mixture of nitrogen of the air with water vapor and carbon dioxide at high temperature. Expanding gas and heat created great pressure. This caused gases to pass through the tubes with enormous velocity.

The *Wing* had proved capable of a speed of more than five hundred miles an hour.

Doc Savage's helpers had made everything ready. The *Wing* was divided into many compartments. Its controls were much the same as those of a dirigible, except the *Wing* could climb, bank and dive with the mobility of the fastest plane.

"At last, you must feel like you're going home," drawled Ham. He was talking to Monk. "Hey, for the love of Pete! I thought you'd left that shote behind this time!"

"Habeas Corpus would feel lonesome without having your yap to listen to," announced Monk.

The ornate, chromium-lined pen he was putting aboard the *Wing* contained the long-eared, long-legged Australian hog.

"I don't feel I should leave New York without knowing more of what happened to Prince Zaban's body," said Count Cardoti.

"There is nothing can be done now about Prince Zaban's corpse," stated Doc Savage. "If the police discover it, I have arranged for the commissioner to make immediate radio contact with our craft. After all, it may be the police will never find the body."

The wide doors of the *Wing*'s dock swung slowly open. Doc had placed Count Cardoti and his companions where they could best observe what would be a rapid ascent above Manhattan.

The man of bronze swung on direct lighting beams which shot in wide fingers across the Hudson. The interior of the warehouse hangar was itself brightly illuminated.

Thuck! Thuck! Thuck! Thuck!

THE drumming beat of wooden paddles hitting the sides of high-prowed war canoes swung the strangely primitive craft directly into the beams.

The canoes were fantastic. Queer figures of native gods and fetishes were carved on the tall prows. The keels were the hollowed trunks of single trees. Above these were bound thinner sides, secured by touch bark fibre.

The warriors were tall and almost naked. Around their arms and throats were pounds of shining copper wire. The loops of their ears swung hideously free.

An upright figure in the bow of one canoe was shouting. The *Wing* had not started to move. The helpers were preparing to cast off the mooring lines. The explosions of the tubes would shoot the aircraft onto the river with the speed of a rocket.

Doc Savage was cautiously picking out a pathway in which no river craft might be lying.

From the hand of the weird figure in the bow of the leading canoe hurtled a long spear. Its ostrich feathers trailed. The weapon was ridiculous. Its blade fell short of touching the gleaming alloy metal of the *Wing*.

The native spear, hurled at perhaps the world's most advanced aërial machine, was no more ludicrous than the giant figure in the prow of the canoe. Tufts of white ostrich feathers denoted his status.

The man was a chief. As such, he was a sort of *Ras*. This meant he was royalty of a sorts. While his warriors were weirdly adorned, the chief went them one better.

The hideous loops of the chief's ears seemed to dance. In one loop was a can of condensed milk. The other loop contained no less than a can of condensed beef.

Doc Savage gave a signal. His helpers stuck by the mooring lines. The first of the long canoes was directly in the pathway of the *Wing*. The man of bronze could have annihilated the natives. He did not wish to do this.

Thuck! Thuck! Thuck! Thuck! The paddles of the second canoe beat in rhythm. The hard heel of a hand pounded on a skin drum.

Flames like small torches danced in the water. The warriors in the second canoe let out a yell. Arcs of fire arose. They were shooting flaming arrows into the opening of the old warehouse.

Some of the arrows struck in tinderlike wood. Smudgy blazes started. Hangar helpers ran with fire extinguishers. But the arrows had become a cloud. Fire was breaking out in several spots.

Count Cardoti shouted, "They'll burn us alive before we can get out of here!"

LED by their prancing chief with the cans in his ears, the crew of one canoe was scrambling onto the wharf of the hangar dock. Monk and Johnny sprang from the *Wing*. They carried the superfiring pistols with drums of mercy bullets.

The machine pistols whanged like swarms of angry bees. The dazed warriors dropped their spears and fell. They were overcome instantly by the anaesthetic of the mercy bullets. The chief jumped back into the canoe.

One of the cans fell out of an ear loop. This seemed to discourage the chief. The whooping mercy pistols had virtually wiped out the warriors of the one canoe. The chief then proved he was of a royal strain.

As a *Ras* of the wild Masai, he was disgraced. In the language of America, he couldn't take it. With a wild cry, the chief flung himself forward. His short, stabbing spear was in his hand. The broad sharp blade pierced his breast.

With a final gulping cry, the chief committed himself to the Long Juju or whatever other gods he might have had in mind. The body splashed and sank.

The front of the warehouse was flaming. The warriors continued to shoot flaming arrows. They varied these with small darts from short blowpipes. A dart struck one of the hangar helpers. The man fell instantly.

"Get aboard," Doc ordered. "We must bring this to an end or more lives will be lost."

A sheet of fire whipped across between the *Wing* and the open river. The Masai backed on their paddles. Their canoe slid out of the blaze.

WITH Monk and Johnny aboard, Doc Savage touched a lever. The result was like the sudden whistling of a mighty wind in a cavern.

The *Wing* moved with a darting suddenness that hurled Count Cardoti from his position. Doc's men had braced themselves for the shock. The *Wing* immediately whipped off the water.

Had the tons of the streamlined aircraft hit the canoe, nothing would have remained but small splinters and shredded flesh.

"Howlin' calamities!" squawked Monk. "The warehouse is going up in smoke! It'll take all the planes an' the subs!"

Doc Savage said nothing.

The magical, bronze hands played over the multiple controls of the *Wing*. It lifted as suddenly as an eagle dropping from a high peak. A peculiar thing happened to the remaining war canoe of the Masai.

"Good grief!" rapped out Ham. "I've heard of ships being blown out of water, but never anything like that!"

The man of bronze had deliberately directed the terrific blast of the propelling gases upon the canoe as the *Wing* passed over it. The quaintly carved craft of the Masai lifted like a feather caught in a cyclone.

As the canoe whirled over in midair, the nearly naked warriors spilled grotesquely into the murky Hudson.

"The hangar's going up in smoke!" yelled Monk again.

Then even Doc's men were silenced. Doc must have stood the *Wing* on one of its tips. It hovered like a hawk about to drop on a fish or a field mouse. From its tubes roared the tremendous blast of the gases of propulsion.

Having already burned in the combustion chamber, the thunderous explosion was like a mighty, driving piston of compressed air. It had the same effect as the slipstream of an airplane on the ground, only its power was perhaps a thousand times greater.

The front wall of the warehouse collapsed. Some of the men inside were hurled from their feet. But the fire was extinguished instantly. It was like a giant's breath blowing out a match.

Suddenly the partly burned warehouse was dropping away. The Hudson River, the spilled Masai canoe and the lights of other water craft fell back.

"WHEW!" gasped Count Cardoti. "I would never have believed such power existed! It's like being blown up on a leaf in a whirlwind!"

In the blast of its own power, the *Wing* was much like a single leaf. Only Doc Savage had complete control of its course. The ascent to ten thousand feet was like the rush of a rocket. The man of bronze touched a stabilizing device.

The *Wing* glided over the glittering skyscrapers of Manhattan at tremendous speed.

Doc Savage was setting a course somewhat south of the Great Circle crossing, used by both ordinary aircraft and ships. When necessary, he would send the *Wing* to an altitude unaffected by the currents of wind closer to the earth's surface.

"We shall be somewhere over Africa shortly after dawn," announced Doc.

"It is incomprehensible," stated Count Cardoti. "Why, with a machine such as this, the fastest pursuit ships and the most powerful modern bombers would be rendered helpless!"

The man of bronze said nothing. Possibly he might have had something of the same thought.

"Listen, ape, you put that confounded shote back where he belongs or he's going to make a jump without any 'chute!"

rapped out Ham. "I've stood for a lot, but this is too much!"

Monk emitted a howl of delight. Habeas Corpus had discovered a new way to torment the irascible Ham. While the lawyer had been looking at the vanishing lights of Manhattan, the rough tongue of the pig had been busy.

He had removed most of the polish from Ham's carefully shined shoes. Habeas Corpus bared his teeth and waved his ears. He was grinning at Ham, if a pig could be said to grin.

Count Cardoti was looking at the mass of equipment inside the *Wing.*

"If King Udu had you for an army, he would scarcely need any other force to retain his kingdom," announced Count Cardoti. "It is to be regretted that King Udu must soon pass away and leave his kingdom to the ignorant prejudices of the wilder tribes."

Doc Savage said nothing. If he had spoken, he would have said that Count Cardoti had voiced what he had in mind. If King Udu proved to be the worthy ruler he was represented by Renny to be, then the monarch of Kokoland might have Doc Savage and his men for an "army."

THE interior of the *Wing* was as steady as if the occupants had been standing on solid ground. Special stabilizing aërolons compensated for the worst of the air pockets. At the terrific speed of nearly five hundred miles an hour, such pockets had almost ceased to exist.

"I feel we are leaving several matters in a tangled condition," commented Count Cardoti. "I realize the importance of reaching Kokoland, but I would have liked to learn more about what happened to the body of Prince Zaban. And I am greatly worried about your cousin, Miss Savage. There seems to be something sinister about this Señorita Moncarid."

"Pat usually can take care of herself," stated Doc. "About the body of Prince Zaban, you yourself said it would be highly important for the prince to be buried in his own country, with the proper tribal rites. Then, if it should happen a successor to King Udu could be discovered, the kingdom might be continued."

"If even that could be true," said Count Cardoti, "you forget the Blood Idol which seems to be missing. I am beginning to believe that whatever this fetish may be, King Udu's rule would be overthrown without it."

"I have not forgotten the Blood Idol," advised Doc. "And

I have been somewhat concerned about the safety of my cousin. However, several queer circumstances may have arisen."

Monk interrupted with a cry from the rear of the *Wing* cabin. Here were a number of doors leading into side compartments. Monk had opened one of these doors.

"Dag-gonit, Doc!" he exclaimed in his childlike treble. "What I'm seein' ain't possible! Doc! Ham! Johnny!"

The ugly-looking chemist had screwed his hairy face into a knot. His sloping forehead gave him the appearance of a puzzled baboon. He hopped up and down much like one.

"What can it be?" exclaimed Count Cardoti.

"The prince! The prince!" squeaked Monk. "Doc, did you know about this?"

"The idea of going back among his nearest living relatives in the African jungles has been too much for him," murmured Ham. "Doc, we may have to tie him up."

THE *Wing* was now at a height of nearly five miles. The air in the cabin was being supplied by oxygen and nitrogen tanks. Doc turned quietly from the stabilizers.

Count Cardoti followed the others to the small door of the compartment. Inside this an ornate casket stood erect. The plate over the face was opened. The quiet features of Prince Zaban were fully revealed.

Count Cardoti sputtered wildly.

"Mr. Savage! How in the world could this have happened? The body was seized—Mr. Savage—you couldn't have known—"

"I did know," stated Doc calmly. "The body never was seized. In fact, it was not at any time in the funeral procession. I decided it might be best to see that Prince Zaban was returned to Kokoland."

Count Cardoti was staring wildly at Doc. He recovered quickly.

"You are remarkably wise, Mr. Savage," he stated. "No other living man would ever have thought of such a clever ruse. Yet you could not have known the funeral procession might be attacked. At the time, you were somewhere else."

"I happened to be driving the funeral car in the cortege," advised Doc. "I imagined there were those who would want to make sure Prince Zaban's body did not get back to his own land."

Count Cardoti was about to reply, when he let out a strangled cry.

"Look! Look! The coffin is moving—it's falling!"

The casket was slowly toppling forward. It was as if some force behind were pushing it. Monk and Johnny sprang inside the compartment. They caught the weight before it struck.

"It's Pat!" exploded Monk. "Pat herself, back in there!"

"This is indeed a most weird materialization," stated the long-worded Johnny. "If it is not an hallucination, Patricia has company."

"Oh, Doc! Please don't look like that!" came Pat Savage's voice. "I just knew you wouldn't let us accompany you, so there didn't seem to be any other way!"

Count Cardoti's black eyes gleamed with appreciation at the lovely Pat. This remarkable young woman's face was flushed and dirty. Pat had a remarkable faculty for getting her face dirty. It only seemed to add to her beauty.

"I instructed you to go home," stated Doc Savage. "You not only have stowed away, but you have taken the liberty to bring others."

"Yes—yes—I brought them—but when you know, you can't do anything but take us with you!" stammered Pat.

"I can still reverse our direction," stated Doc. "We would lose only a little time."

"No—no—please, Doc!" exclaimed Pat. "This is Señorita Moncarid, and this is—"

"The man representing himself to be William Smith of 4404 Crooked Neck Road, Long Island," interrupted the man of bronze. "But known to King Udo of Kokoland as Logo."

"Well, I'll be superamalgamated!" exclaimed Johnny.

The African with the thin, arched nose, beside the lovely Señorita Moncarid, was the chauffeur who had been driving her car when Pat Savage had entered it.

Chapter XI

LAND OF LONG JUJU

THE *Wing* of Doc Savage hovered over a great mountain at dawn.

Great Mount Kibo was a floating cloud of mist. Its 19,800 feet of bulk presented one of the strangest spectacles of the equatorial tropics.

This highest peak of the Kilimanjaro Range rose from the steamy swelter of matted jungles to the cold, stark rocks of the snow.

High on its plains played the *kudu,* or great antelope. But at its feet the great beasts of the Tertiary Age still haunted its lower regions. Hippopotamuses abounded in the lakes and swamps.

Across the Kilimanjaro plains the *simba,* the lion, sent its fear-inspiring roar at night. Leopard, hyena, cheetah and jackal prowled in its secluded places.

"It's the world as it was before the flood of Noah," announced the learned Johnny. "It seems the deluge never reached the heights of the Kilimanjaro."

Doc Savage's marvelous flying *Wing* was at the time suspended over a remarkable vista. Here, in 1848, the first German missionary had found a gleaming cone of snow, rising almost from the equator. He was awed by the unexpected beauty and majesty of the peaks.

The world got a book, written to prove there could be no snow near the equator. It was said the missionary had seen a mirage. His story was not believed until 1860.

Because of its sustaining gas, the *Wing* could be held almost stationary. Below, was all the panorama of Central East Africa. The dense Taveta Forest stretched southward toward the blue-ridged Parri Mountains.

"Within the region between these mountains are the forty

or more tribes of King Udu's Kokoland, the richest monarchy in Africa," said Count Cardoti. "And it is to this country we have, through Mr. Savage, the great honor of returning my poor friend, Prince Zaban, for the proper tribal burial."

Count Cardoti was speaking to Pat Savage. The dark eyes of Señorita Moncarid observed him closely. Señorita Moncarid talked little. She had admitted to Pat Savage that she had at one time been a Masai. A Spanish family had been attracted by her beauty.

Señorita Moncarid had been spirited away to Spain. Later, she had been educated in the United States. Tribal marks of the Masai tribe had been eliminated by good surgery.

Count Cardoti had calmly accepted the surprise of accompanying Prince Zaban's body back to Kokoland.

Doc Savage now was observing many miles of the country.

"Dag-gonit!" complained Monk. "Renny's down in all that smother somewhere!"

Doc had been trying to pick up Renny's transmitter. He had met with no success.

"I have heard of The Shimba," Count Cardoti told Doc Savage. "Only the warriors who had killed man-eating lions with their spears are permitted to wear the mane and head of a lion. I fancy this one they call The Shimba is some renegade white man."

Doc Savage said nothing of his own belief. The first few hours had been spent reconnoitering the mountain region.

Now Doc Savage was employing powerful binoculars of four dimensional lenses. These not only brought distant objects closer, they made them stand out in stereoscopic detail. A low, fantastic trilling came from the man of bronze.

Far below the snow line south of the Kilimanjaro, was what had the appearance of still more snow. Down there, north of the range, separated from Kokoland by a narrow, high-walled mountain pass, a small army was camped. The expanse of white was a double line of grounded war planes.

Beyond these white planes lay a wide splotch of what might have been black snow. But this black was the color of the tents of the country.

"I would say," observed Doc Savage, "that we have arrived none too soon. The Northern Legion, of which Renny told us, seems preparing to strike. In addition to fifty or more bombing planes, the army has four war tanks. The activity would indicate they are preparing for movement through the mountain pass to the southward."

Count Cardoti exclaimed over the clearness with which the high-powered binoculars revealed the army camps.

"It would seem as if those chaps were looking directly at us!"

"Yeah, and if they were, we wouldn't be hanging around here for long," replied Ham. "Doc, what are your plans?"

"First, I would place Prince Zaban's body in a secure spot," said Doc. "We will then see if we can locate Renny's *safari*."

FAR below, the invaders were unaware their movements were being observed. The one camp was of foot soldiers and the tanks. These were all that could be employed for attack in the jungle wilderness of Kokoland.

Doc Savage's study revealed the army to be made up of representatives of serveral nations, a freebooters' legion.

"If I were King Udu, I would deploy my forces so strategically they could not be touched by bombs from above," commented the astute Johnny.

"That is a thought to remember," stated Count Cardoti. "Only I fear King Udu is too old, and too ill, to be of much account in directing his armies."

The equatorial sun seemed to be rolling along the rim beyond the mountains. It painted the jungles in myriad colors. The *Wing* was again beyond the ground vision of the encamped invaders.

"When darkness has come, we will descend and observe if there are plans for immediate movement," stated Doc.

The *Wing* had descended once. The body of Prince Zaban was hidden securely in a niche in the mountains. During the afternoon there had been faint stuttering static on Doc's radio finder.

Doubtless this had been Renny trying to make contact. Perhaps the big engineer might even have observed the *Wing* through his own high-powered binoculars.

The sun was on the horizon. Though the *Wing* was miles high, the sun sank as abruptly as if it had been pulled away by a giant hand.

"Oh!" exclaimed Pat Savage. "I've never seen anything more beautiful!"

"Or more likely to be deadly," observed Ham. "If some of those air scouts down there take a notion to go sky hunting, we may have our hands full."

"It is hardly likely they would find us," said Count Cardoti.

The *Wing* was merged with the milky brightness of the tropical, star-studded sky. Its greatest advantage was its lack of vibration or motor impact. At cruising speed, the compound mixture was only a hissing through the tubes, which could not have been picked up by airplane detectors.

"King Udu has two obsolete planes, a couple of rickety Spads of the World War period," Count Cardoti informed Doc Savage. "If they ever get off the ground, they'll be more dangerous for their own fliers than for the enemy."

"I wish we could get in touch with Renny," complained Ham for the twentieth time. "I'm afraid something has happened to him."

"If he really encountered The Shimba, as you believe, then he is in the gravest danger," declared Count Cardoti. "The Shimba, as I have been told, never lets up on any one who has beaten him once."

"Dag-gonit!" boasted Monk. "The Shimba may be something, but if he ever gets in front of Renny's fists, he'll need something more than bum magic!"

SURROUNDED by tropical darkness, Doc Savage determined to become better informed of the number of the foreign white men and of their possible movements. Suddenly the *Wing* was dropping with a speed that caused Count Cardoti and Señorita Moncarid to draw in deep breaths.

It seemed as if the *Wing* had suddenly lost all of its sustaining gas.

"If you will put on the infra-red goggles, you may be able to observe what our friends below are doing," advised Doc Savage.

Señorita Moncarid gasped with wonder. It was her first experience with the high lights of the infra-red rays. Through the huge goggles, she was looking down on a strange spectacle.

The squadron of planes was clearly revealed, as if in a motion picture still. So were the grim army tanks. Among them several hundred men were moving about. It was clear they were preparing for some action.

"This gives us a clear conception of their position and the

route they must follow to enter the pass," stated Doc Savage.

Abruptly, the vibration detector on the instrument board of the *Wing* itself began oscillating. From the machine came a low humming.

"They've got a plane up!" exclaimed Ham. "We'd better have a look around!"

"None of the legion planes have left the ground," advised Doc. "There are eleven pursuit planes and eighteen bombers."

Count Cardoti took in the bronze man with a look of wonderment. He would have been more amazed if he had known that Doc Savage could have told him accurately, at this moment, the exact number of men in the camps, and the extent of their equipment and ammunition. He also had ascertained some of the invaders were Asiatics.

Doc Savage had dropped the *Wing* to a low level. At this spot they were hedged in by high ridges. Clearly now, came the drumming of a plane somewhere overhead.

Doc tuned in the observation lens. Into it rocketed a single plane of an obsolete pattern. In the television arrangement, the plane's wings trembled as if they were about to drop off.

"It's one of King Udu's shaky Spads!" exclaimed Count Cardoti.

FROM the ground below shot a plane detector beam. It enveloped the *Wing* and the Spad in spreading illumination. Immediately men poured from the tents like black ants from hills. Brass guns gleamed suddenly.

Fire spouted. Incendiary tracer bullets painted a line toward the *Wing* and the shaky, old Spad. Doc Savage could have shot the *Wing* to a safe height within a few seconds. Instead, the man of bronze flattened the *Wing*.

"They've got our range!" shouted Ham. "I can feel them smacking the undercarriage!"

Slugs of the anti-aircraft stream were hammering at the lower part of the *Wing*. Some of the tracer bullets found the Spad. The edge of one of its wings went ragged with a bursting explosion.

The radiant beam from the ground showed the face of a scared native flier.

"Shouldn't we get out of this before they hit some vital part?" questioned Count Cardoti.

"Thunderation!" spouted Monk. "That's one thing this *Wing* hasn't got! There ain't any vital parts!"

"They can do us no damage," advised Doc. "They are now using their magnetic ray. It will be unfortunate for the plane of King Udu."

The magnetic ray was invisible. The *Wing* remained unaffected. Having no motors operated by electrical ignition, its combustion tubes continued their slow hissing.

"Howlin' calamities!" shouted Monk. "Look out, Doc! The native flier's out of business!"

The magnetic ray was invisible. It had the quality of paralyzing the motor of an airplane. Apparently the engine of the old Spad instantly went dead. The crazy wings flashed into a twisting spin.

"Oh, he'll be crushed to pieces!" cried Pat Savage. "Doc, the plane's going to hit us!"

Doc's quick hands had flattened the great metallic *Wing*. Its broad surface now was directly under the falling Spad.

"Keep the control steady, Johnny!" directed Doc.

The man of bronze had whipped from his seat. He was swinging through an automatic hatchway in the roof of the wing. It seemed as if he would be flattened by the smash of the spinning Spad.

"He'll be killed, and then what will we do?" exclaimed Señorita Moncarid.

The strange woman had spoken but little. Now she was concerned for the safety of the man of bronze. Reared as she had been among the superstitious Masai, the señorita must have believed Doc Savage to be some sort of a god.

PERHAPS the terror-stricken flier of the King Udu plane also believed he had encountered some unknown god of the air. Probably he had been resigned to take the death crash. The old Spad carried no parachute. The exploding bullets had broken its wings. The magnetic ray had killed its motor.

Now the flier was plunging toward the earth. Next, it must have seemed to him that a great, bright-winged monster had interfered. And on the back of that monster appeared a tremendous figure.

As the Spad crumpled into the metallic surface of the *Wing*, Doc Savage leaped. One steel-strong hand gripped the rim of the Spad's cockpit. The other hand fastened on the shoulder of the dazed flier.

The grip of the bronze fingers was tremendous. They sank into the flesh until blood slowly oozed.

On the terrain below, amazed airmen and soldiers witnessed an unbelievable episode. The crumpled old Spad whirled down upon them. Its weight crashed into one of the black tents.

The Spad contained no flier. No man had been seen to fall in the beam still playing steadily upon the strange *Wing*.

The *Wing* was still so low that machine guns were turned upon it. The pounding stream of bullets caused no damage. The mysterious *Wing* turned like a lazy, scornful monster. It went hissing upward.

Doc Savage slipped into the *Wing*'s cabin through the sliding hatchway. The native flier fell on his knees. He pulled a killing knife from the broad hide belt wrapped around his middle. Slowly he placed the rounded edge over his stomach.

One hand caught Doc Savage's wrist. The lips pressed the back of the bronze man's hand. The arched-nosed William Smith, or Logo, sprang to the man's side. He spoke to him rapidly in Kokonese.

"He says he is forever the slave of the god, *B'wana* Savage," explained Logo.

"Tell him to arise and explain to you what the situation may be in King Udu's kingdom," directed Doc. "Inquire if a big white man with a gloomy face has appeared?"

In the flier's mixed patois of Kokonese and English it seemed the situation in King Udu's village was acute. The people believed King Udu to be dying. The tribes had heard Prince Zaban had been killed and taken away by evil spirits without proper burial. The priests of the Long Juju had become strong.

No white man answering the description of Renny had appeared. Masai and Swahili warriors, led by the mystic Shimba, had been stealing women and children. They had practically surrounded King Udu's palace.

Chapter XII

THE KING IS DYING

"SUMMING it all up," stated Ham, "it would seem our King Udu is having his share of trouble. What do you suppose has become of Renny, Doc?"

"Perhaps Renny is remaining in a safe position, where he can observe affairs until our arrival," stated Doc. "We shall move at once to the king's village."

In spite of its tremendous power, contrary winds around the Kilimanjaro Range hampered the flight of the *Wing*. Following the crash of the Spad, the European Legion had got half a dozen pursuit ships into the air.

Count Cardoti polished his finger nails nervously. A dozen beams of light flashed around the *Wing*. Doc Savage apparently made no effort to avoid the pursuers.

"It would be as well perhaps that they now learn to be cautious," stated Doc.

Señorita Moncarid's eyes sparkled.

"I have never seen any one so wonderful as your great cousin," she said to Pat Savage. "He is what you call—invincible."

Pat merely nodded and smiled. At this moment machine gun bullets had begun hammering the *Wing*, like rain on a tin roof. They had about as much effect upon its bulletproof composition. The crystal alloy glass of its observation windows did not show so much as the trace of a spider crack.

This new composition had been perfected by Monk, directed by Doc. The old bulletproof glass with its spreading spider tracks had been annoying.

Doc flew the *Wing* steadily southward. He had discovered a nook in the mountain range, where no plane of regular construction could have possibly landed. Even a close approach would have been prevented by the furious updraft of the mountain wind. It was in this place the casket containing the body of Prince Zaban had been concealed.

THE pursuit planes darted around like angry hornets. One bomber made an attempt to attack the mysterious craft. The man of bronze avoided it easily. Each time the bomber moved into position for a possible dropping of explosive, the *Wing* sideslipped.

Suddenly there was a yell from Monk.

"Doc! That crazy guy's tryin' to commit suicide!"

The apelike chemist had been closely observing the pursuit planes. One flier had separated from the others. He had zoomed suddenly for height. Now he was coming down in a full power, screaming dive. The shrieking of his propeller could be heard above the low hissing of the *Wing*.

Suicide was the exact word. The flier might have been obeying a death order.

Doc Savage manipulated the controls. The *Wing* banked, started to roll. But the pursuit ship was like a darting arrow. Its silvery nose crashed in almost the exact middle of the stiff metal of the *Wing*.

"We're going down!" shouted Count Cardoti. "I knew they would get us, if we kept on fooling around!"

Escaping gas let out a loud hissing. Fortunately, the *Wing* was constructed for just such an emergency. Its sustaining gas was contained in separate compartments.

In the roof of the *Wing* a dead, mangled flier lay in his smashed plane. Flame shot up from his cockpit. The aviator had been even greater than a mere suicide. He had used his brain as well as his life in an effort to wipe the *Wing* out of the sky.

The man's body was rapidly charring to cinders in his blazing plane. The pursuit ship was locked tightly in the metal of the *Wing*. Fortunately, it was not in contact with any part which might have been set afire.

Only, the weight and position of the wreckage hampered operation of the controls.

The *Wing* was sinking toward the jagged teeth of the range which extended east and west from Mount Kibo.

"Perhaps all had better put on the parachutes." advised Doc Savage. "The mountain has many perils."

THOUGH it was crippled, the *Wing* was kept circling by the marvelous skill of Doc Savage. His bronze hands played on the controls. He jockeyed for a safer position in the sky, near the ragged range of the mountain. Other pursuit ships were withdrawing.

They must have believed they had witnessed the finish of their terrible, mysterious visitor. For the flames from the burning plane, locked in the metal top, made it appear that all of the *Wing* was blazing.

Mount Kibo with its hungry blasts was too perilous a spot into which to venture needlessly. The great *Wing* flashed out of sight in the night mist. Then it became only a dull flare behind the serrated range.

No doubt the pursuit fliers believed their fellow flier's death had accomplished its purpose. Surely none could be left alive when the falling aircraft crashed.

But Doc had brought the *Wing* safely to earth.

"He was a brave man and deserving of a better fate," stated Doc Savage.

Thus the man of bronze paid tribute to the flier who had burned in the wreckage of his plane, atop the grounded *Wing*. The plane was removed. Monk and Ham were repairing the damaged gas compartment.

"Johnny, you will remain with the *Wing*," directed Doc Savage. "We will make our way to the village of King Udu."

The man of bronze had brought the *Wing* back to the sheltered gorge, where the body of Prince Zaban had been concealed. Now a strange funeral procession made ready to move overland to the palace of the ruler of Kokoland.

The foreign casket was borne on the brawny shoulders of Logo and the flier who had been snatched by Doc Savage from death in the sky.

The descent to the thicker and warmer bush of the jungle was a trying march. Señorita Moncarid and Pat Savage were enwrapped in heavy garments. Here at the fourteen-thousand-foot level, were patches of dirty snow.

Something in the night began whistling in cheery fashion. The sound was so remarkably human that Monk halted instantly.

"That is not one of your kinsfolk," observed Ham sarcastically. "The first baboons are much lower down. If I have it correctly, that is a brown stonechat bird."

Pat Savage repressed a little scream as several animals

darted almost under their feet. They were striped like chipmunks, but had the tails of rats.

"Those," said Ham, "are *Rodentis Macqueniensis*." He hastily added, "Johnny told me their names. They are field rats to you, Monk."

A FEW thousand feet below Mount Kibo, moist heat took the place of the sharp air above. Logo, and the other native carrying the casket of Prince Zaban, sweated.

This modern casket, one of the finest New York City could produce, afforded a marked contrast to the steaming jungle. The Colobus monkeys were highly excited.

The homely Monk was followed by Habeas Corpus.

"Looks like you've come to a place where you'll have to give up that shote," drawled Ham, with a sarcastic grin. "You've got to make up your mind about one or the other."

"Dag-gonit!" yelped hairy Monk. "Whatcha talkin' about, shyster?"

"I think some of your monkey cousins would like to visit with you," grinned Ham, "only they can't make up their minds what kind of an insect that thing is following you."

Count Cardoti had been silent for some time. He had stayed close by Pat Savage. Now he spoke to Doc Savage.

"I had almost forgotten," said Count Cardoti. "The teakwood block, that package in New York, did you have any report after it was stolen?"

"I had no report after it was stolen from me," replied Doc.

Ham, the lawyer, smiled to himself. The bronze man had spoken the exact truth. It was what Ham would have termed a legal evasion.

At this moment Ham also was wondering. Events had come so swiftly that the curious teakwood box had apparently been forgotten. Doc Savage had said it contained a priceless jewel.

Ham knew the marvelous brain of the bronze man never overlooked even a trivial detail. The teakwood box was more than that. Doc had said they must guard the contents of the box with their lives.

The box had not been stolen from Doc. It had been replaced in the big safe, before the interrupted funeral of Prince Zaban. Ham could not recall the teakwood box having been removed to the *Wing*.

And if it had been, where now was the mysterious block with its lid that would open only at the impulse of an electroscopic ray?

Even Ham and Monk, aware of the ways of Doc Savage, would have been amazed to know the teakwood block was very close to them. At the time Count Cardoti asked the question concerning a report on the theft of the package from Doc's safe, the teakwood block was moving toward the palace of King Udu.

MORE than the Colobus monkeys, more than the chattering of the baby-voiced hyrax squirrels disturbed the jungle, as Doc Savage's small *safari* moved into the heart of Kokoland.

Tunk-tunk-tunk-tunk!

From hilltop to hilltop, spaced messages were being tapped.

This was the rapid thumping of the tight skin over the ends of hollow logs. Doc Savage knew the eyes of the jungle were now fixed upon the little procession. Count Cardoti glanced about apprehensively.

"King Udu already knows we have arrived," he stated. "I fear also that others much less friendly have been informed."

Tunk-tunk-tunk-tunk!

The swift telegraph of the bush was telling its story.

Doc Savage only hoped none of the spies of the wild tribes had been far enough up Mount Kibo to have observed the landing of the *Wing*. Detection now would make it tough for Johnny, who was alone on guard.

The man of bronze was not, however, so greatly worried about the geologist. The *Wing* was equipped with several automatic devices. The approach of enemies would bring the release of stupefying gases. Other weird manifestations would doubtless frighten away superstitious natives.

Not a liana vine moved. There appeared to be no life in this lower jungle. The splashing of beasts in occasional water-holes was missing. This of itself was most ominous.

For the drums continued talking.

Doc Savage was well aware the body of Prince Zaban had more than their own small escort. Half-naked figures were weaving through the jungle bush. Eyes surrounded by white circles of ochre no doubt were fixed on the ornate casket of gleaming plush and silver, borne on the shoulders of Logo and the other native.

"I don't like this at all," complained Monk. "It is suddenly too quiet. I wish they would stop pounding them drums."

Doc Savage suspected an attack might have been made upon the small party except for one thing. The eyes observing them were conveying a weird message to primitive brains.

The message passing from drum to drum may have been of the arrival of a new god in the land of the Kilimanjaro. The concealed natives must have believed the ornate casket could bear only gifts to such a god, or perhaps the great fetish itself.

And at this time, King Udu was receiving word of the visitors with their strange burden.

KING UDU reclined on a couch of spotted leopard skins. Long, white hair fell about massive shoulders. The shoulders were great, even though they now sagged.

For King Udu was of tremendous weight. Though in the late nineties, the ruler was still enormously fat. His faded eyes peered out over three rolling chins.

King Udu moved his pudgy hands feebly. On nearly all of his fingers flashed jewels of many colors, but crudely cut.

But fat as he was, King Udu's nose was thin and highly arched.

"What do you see, Selan?" questioned the king in a weak voice.

Before the monarch squatted a grotesquely thin figure on bony haunches. He had all the decorations of a tribal medicine man. His head was shaved and polished.

"They are evil ones," intoned the medicine man. "They are bearing a shining box. In it may be destruction."

Plainly, Selan did not approve of the coming of what might be some new form of witchcraft. His face was long and twisted into countless wrinkles. He wore a heavy scowl as he replied to King Udu.

Though Doc Savage and his companions were still some distance in the jungle, the village of King Udu was marking the approach. More than twenty tribes were represented in the thick dust of the streets.

King Udu had ordered a mobilization of all his people. He had attempted to quell an uprising of the wild Masai and the Swahili. The threat of the mysterious Shimba had caused terror among those of the more peaceful tribes.

Word had come of the assembling of an European and Asiatic army beyond the mountains. Messengers had been sent with demands upon King Udu.

"The radio box has informed me we must prepare for action," said King Udu. "What has Selan to advise? Should we send out an army to meet these foreign devils? Or should we scatter to the hills?"

As King Udu's hand waved, his togalike *chamma* draped over his slumped figure. This snow-white, cotton garment, hitched over the rolling shoulders, was an Abyssinian mark of royalty. Only the archives of the family of King Udu knew how this distinguishing garment had come into the Kilimanjaro Mountain country, more than eight lifetimes before.

"Great King," intoned Selan, the medicine man, wagging his bare skull and frowning deeply into his many wrinkles. "The invaders are too strong. The time may have come to yield. The successor to the throne is no longer living. The Blood Idol has been sent away. Many of our people are afraid."

A SCORE of nearly naked chanters sat in a row, in what King Udu evidently called his throne room. Now his only throne was the couch of skins on which he was forced to recline.

The raftered walls of the king's palace afforded strange contrasts.

On one side of King Udu's couch of skins were weird, smiling heads. Hundreds of these were stuck upon teakwood pegs driven into walls of palmetto thatch. They were the skulls of enemies slain by King Udu's head-hunting tribes.

These tribal trophies must remain close to the throne, if Udu was to continue his domination of all his blood-thirsty chiefs.

Beyond the couch loomed a contrasting apparatus. This was no less than one of the most modern of radios. Beside this was a glass square.

The wise and advanced King Udu had even attempted to have television installed. This had never worked as it should.

At one end of the huge room was an airplane. True, it was only an obsolete old Spad from the World War.

But it was a plane. And every part was kept polished.

Outside in the streets of the village, the natives of several tribes were chanting, dancing or gathered in subdued groups.

One tribe circled, waving long spears to the tuneless thumping of tom-toms.

The Kokonese, King Udu's own people, seemed to be attempting to drill with a few guns.

In King Udu's palace were six very old men. They sat in a row behind Selan, the chief counselor. The six counselors to the king were worried and solemn.

DRILLING of the natives in the street abruptly ceased. They gazed with superstitious fear at the figure of the bronze Doc Savage, who had come striding into the village. Logo walked with head erect, helping bear the casket of silver and black.

Logo rapped out sharp words in Kokonese.

"Prince Zaban has come home!"

Many tribesmen prostrated themselves. The drilling Kokonese bowed their heads and muttered. Drums started beating in dirgelike cadence. Voices of warriors and women wailed in time with the drums.

"Some homecoming for the prince!" observed Monk.

"We will do well for the moment to make no observations," advised Doc Savage.

"Meaning for you to shut your trap, ape," growled Ham. "Maybe that shote of yours is worth something."

Ham referred to the long-eared, grotesque Habeas Corpus. The smart pig stuck close to Monk's heels.

Many of the natives of the flat noses, those from the farther hills, must have been impressed by the Australian hog.

Doc Savage had taken in all of the fantastic village. Every manner of grass hut and thatched, bamboo building known to the various tribes appeared on different streets.

The man of bronze noted the separate establishments for the women of the Kokonese. He spoke with Patricia Savage.

"It is against the custom of the people for women to appear before the king," stated Doc. "You will accompany Señorita Moncarid to the long hut of the women. There you will be safe enough."

"Well, I like that!" exclaimed Pat Savage, viewing the long hut in which many women were gabbling. "You think I came all the way to Africa to be stuck with a bunch of women?"

"As I recall it, you were not especially invited to come to Africa," said Doc calmly. "We will see that you have some of the more modern comforts if that is possible."

"It is the custom of the people, Miss Savage," interjected Señorita Moncarid. "It is only when we are requested, that we may appear before the king or one of the royal chiefs."

"That is true, Miss Savage," agreed Count Cardoti. "As soon as we have concluded the necessary interview with King Udu, I will see about a separate establishment."

MONK gasped at the fantastic array inside the throne room of King Udu. The chanters, Selan, the medicine man, and the six solemn counselors gazed with awe on the giant figure of Doc Savage.

The clear bronze skin, the flaky gold eyes and the smooth golden mask of Doc's hair must have given him the appearance of some sort of a god. Even Selan, who partly ruled King Udu by virtue of his position, mumbled humbly before the bronze giant.

King Udu spoke in the best of English.

"I appreciate your coming, Doc Savage, the great one," he said. "*B'wana* Renwick had informed me of some of your powers. The bringing home of my only son places me enormously in your debt. First of all you make possible the necessary tribal ceremony. But I fear your arrival is too late. I have not many days, Doc Savage."

"No man's days are finished until they are all counted," stated Doc Savage. "We will do what we can. Count Cardoti has told me much of your problem."

King Udu attempted to rise from his couch of skins. But the aged monarch fell back heavily and gasped.

"I am grateful indeed to Count Cardoti for his companionship with my poor son," he said, when he could speak. "My people had hoped Zaban would return with much of the wisdom of the white man to rule over them. Count Cardoti has done his work well."

"I would advise," stated Doc, "that during the days the body of the prince must repose in state, the casket be opened only for the glimpse of his face."

"That shall be so ordered," agreed King Udu.

The old king called Doc Savage and Count Cardoti close to his couch.

"The influence of witchcraft and the Long Juju has become too strong for my people," he murmured. "Since my son has been murdered, there is none to carry forward. My many chiefs know this. Listen!"

IN the dusty streets of the fantastic village, the beat of many drums suddenly increased. The *tunk-tunk-tunk-tunk* had become a deep throbbing. The dirgelike chant of mourning was rising higher.

The voices in the many dialects of the tribesmen were shrilling into a threat. At one end of the village a weird war dance had been started.

"They would not have a chance against these armed invaders, when they come through the mountain pass," declared King Udu. "My Masai and Swahili have deserted to the Long Juju. The foreign devils await only my death to enslave my people. The Masai and the Swahili will join them in bringing back slavery, the hunting of heads, cannibalism. Even the treasure—the great—"

Old King Udu slumped into the skins of the couch, gasping.

Some of the chanters began a high wailing. This was a cry, which informed those outside King Udu was dead. Though the King was not dead, the sudden cry was disastrous.

Mingled tribesmen suddenly jammed the low doorways of the fantastic throne room. Their wails joined those of the excited chanters.

The massive figure of Doc Savage suddenly stood before the figures of the tribal chiefs. More than a dozen of those with the waving ostrich feathers crowded into the room.

They were amazed to hear this bronze giant speaking abruptly in a mixture of their own tongues. Doc spoke rapidly.

"King Udu has only passed into a dream," said the man of bronze. "In it he will discover what must be done to defeat your enemies."

The jabberings of the chiefs drowned Doc's voice. Tribesmen armed with long spears surged into the room. Selan, the medicine man, spoke sharply. Doc Savage knew Selan had said King Udu was dead.

Perhaps the king's counselor saw opportunity for himself in the passing of the monarchy.

Doc Savage lifted one hand. None saw the tiny object shatter at Selan's bent knees. The chiefs only saw Selan close his eyes and cease speaking. Anæsthetic powder had filled Selan's nostrils.

Doc Savage turned. In the palm of his hand was a small

syringe. But the chiefs saw only the bronze giant's hand pass across King Udu's forehead.

King Udu opened his eyes. His great body lifted. Then he stood on his feet.

The royal chiefs of the tribesmen fell upon their faces.

Chapter XIII

FEAR OF THE PEOPLE

KING UDU's weight was well above three hundred pounds. Amazed counselors, chanters and warrior chiefs saw *Ras* Udu lifted as easily as though he were only a small monkey.

King Udu had stood on his own feet only long enough to make an announcement.

"My chiefs, servants of all the gods!" his voice rolled. "We will not bow before the invading devils! Aid has come to us! We will go before our enemies with our spears sharpened and our heads erect!"

Guttural voices of approval were sounding. King Udu swayed. His strength was leaving his bones.

Doc Savage lifted the weighty king. Lifted him and carried him with ease through the low doorway into the inner room, where Prince Zaban had been placed.

Before this casket, knelt half a dozen weird figures. They were priests with tribal offerings to the dead. At the command of Doc Savage, they arose and departed.

The man of bronze placed King Udu quickly upon another royal couch of skins. Monk and Ham had followed to the doorway.

"Let none enter," commanded Doc. "See that we are undisturbed. Speak to those outside and say King Udu will prepare his plan of defense against his enemies."

Ham and Monk blocked the doorway. Count Cardoti stood in the middle of the throne room. His bright, black eyes gleamed with apparent appreciation.

"Your Doc Savage has by simple magic made it almost possible to set himself up as a successor to *Ras* Udu," he stated.

"Thunderation!" squealed Monk. "Doc wouldn't want any part of this funny place! What could we do here?"

"I don't know what I would do, but any animal with a shape like yours ought to fit in," remarked Ham. "The way things are lining up, we might have to stay longer than we imagine."

"Dag-gonit!" howled Monk. "I suppose you think your brains are too good for this place! I don't like Pat being left out there with all them native women!"

"I have been thinking about that," exclaimed Count Cardoti. "I know these people well. I shall see what arrangements can be made for more exclusive quarters."

Ham and Monk noticed the chiefs of the various tribes moved aside quickly as the dapper figure of Count Cardoti passed. Some bent their heads and touched their foreheads.

"You know," growled Monk, "I believe this count fellow's got the Indian sign on some of these guys."

"No 'count fellow, you mean," snapped Ham. "He does too much thinking about Pat to suit me."

Count Cardoti went through the doorway into the dust of the street. The drums kept up their *tunk-tunking*. Bare feet of the Kokonese shuffled about in their conception of a white man's army drill.

"Howlin' calamities!" exploded Monk. "I'd like to play top sergeant to some of them guys! They'd hotfoot it right or get their toes stepped on!"

"Maybe you'd do better teachin' 'em to swing through the trees," suggested Ham. "That's more in your line."

Neither of the bickering partners realized how soon Monk was to have the opportunity of playing something more than top sergeant to these Kokonese. Nor what a ridiculous figure Ham, once a brigadier general, was to cut in the make-up of the Kokoland army.

At this time it did not seem as if there ever would be an army. Had the invading army found its way through the mountain pass now, there would have been little resistance to its advance.

IN the meantime, King Udu had revived enough to talk with Doc Savage. The ruler of Kokoland was now able to speak only in whispers.

His council of six, and Selan, the chief medicine man, were unable to quiet the fears of the people, King Udu imparted.

"Selan and the others are fearful and their faces are long when they appear before the chiefs," said King Udu. "Only a smile of courage can lead my people to war. My council no longer has courage. Selan and the others have betrayed their fear. The chiefs believe it is my own fear, because my son is dead my days are numbered."

Doc Savage touched the old king's wrist. He felt the weakness of the pulse. Then the bronze man spoke rapidly.

"First, we must discover who is The Shimba," declared Doc. "It is this figure which seems to sway your more superstitious chiefs."

"That I have been unable to discover," whispered King Udu. "Yet from Logo I have learned The Shimba of my own kingdom seemed able to impose his will upon wild tribesmen sent to your great country."

"That would seem to be true," admitted Doc. "Your loyal Logo and his Kokonese helped defeat them. He set a trap with teakwood boxes whereby many were killed. He also assisted in removing the body of Prince Zaban for transportation back to his own country. I am looking deeper into this matter of Señorita Moncarid."

"Yes—yes—" King Udu's voice was very faint. "Señorita Moncarid—it is of peculiar coincidence—the treasure—"

The monarch lapsed into unconsciousness. For the present, Doc Savage judged it best to permit him to rest. The mystery of Señorita Moncarid must wait. Also that of the treasure which King Udu had twice mentioned. Doc now understood the object of the invading army of mixed nationalities. They were adventurers seeking treasure rather than conquest.

The man of bronze stepped into the throne room. Selan had revived. The medicine man was slightly dazed. But it could be seen he was also furiously angry. The council of six had downcast faces.

Selan led in the scowling with which Doc Savage was greeted.

"King Udu is about to depart," asserted Selan. "He has spoken much of your greatness, Doc Savage. But you cannot restore confidence to these many tribes. I shall lead the council in an appeal to the priests of the Long Juju."

Doc Savage surveyed the heavy faces. He could imagine

the six stolid advisors of King Udu were under the power of Selan. The bronze giant's flaky gold eyes held those of smoky black. When he smiled, there were only scowls to answer.

"We will confer shortly," announced Doc. "King Udu will live to see his people victorious. Selan, you and the others will join me presently in the room of eating."

Doc Savage apparently dismissed Selan and his six followers. He turned back to Ham and Monk.

"Where is Count Cardoti?" he inquired.

"Gone to see if he can make arrangements for Pat and Señorita Moncarid to leave the house of the black women," said Ham.

"Count Cardoti must not do that at present," stated Doc. "You will go outside and see that Pat and Señorita Moncarid stay closely with the other women of the Kokonese. There may be grave disturbances soon."

WHEN Doc Savage again faced Selan and the six long-faced black men of King Udu's council in the room of eating, the bronze man was cheerful and smiling.

The man of bronze had spoken with the cooks of the palace. They had set certain delicacies before Selan and the advisors. Among these was one of the land's most appealing dainties.

Perhaps no white man would have appreciated this Kokonese dish. For it was no less than a great pie containing baked white ants. The flavor might have been a little off for a Caucasian palate.

Doc Savage viewed with relish the great pie. He saw that Selan and his scowling followers also appreciated being offered the opportunity for such a feast.

The man of bronze spoke ceremoniously.

"We will add greatly to the flavor of the white ant dish, especially for those of great medicine in the land," he stated.

Doc had placed what resembled a housewife's cream whipper on the long table. Into this he poured goat's cream from a hollowed bamboo. The small machine whirred. The goat's milk was whipped into a frothy mixture.

The man of bronze poured some of the froth on a portion of the white ant pie. He gave every indication of being well pleased with the result.

"It is a dish fit only for the gods," declared Doc. "None

but those of superior medicine should partake of such a delicacy."

The frothy whipped cream ornamented seven portions of the white ant pie. Selan and the others may have been medicine men. They professed to have the power of witch-craft.

But they were no less than hungry children. They wolfed their shares of the white ant pie.

"Good food gives courage for great wars," announced Doc.

It seemed as if mere pie was having that effect. Selan, whose face was the most wrinkled and perhaps the sourest in Kokoland, suddenly widened his toothless mouth in a broad smile.

Others of the six began to crinkle the corners of their jaws. Selan tossed back his polished, bald skull and laughed. At first it was a hideous croaking. It changed to a howl of glee.

The other six looked at him. Their muscles relaxed. They laughed boisterously.

"King Udu is a great king," stated Doc solemnly. "He will live to lead his many peoples to victory."

"He will—will—will—" Selan's wrinkled face contorted, as if with some inner mirth. The ancient medicine man howled with laughter. He was so tickled he choked and couldn't finish the sentence.

The six others agreed with howls.

"King Udu will—King Udu will—"

Tears were rolling down their cheeks. Their ornaments of everything from copper wire to the teeth of the cheetah and the leopard danced and clacked.

Doc Savage arose and led them toward the throne room. He could see many of the tribal chiefs had again assembled. Apparently, they were awaiting word of King Udu's condition.

To the accompaniment of the war drums outside, wild cries were arising.

"What does the king say? Shall it be war? Will King Udu live to lead his army?"

In their various dialects, a score of nearly naked chiefs were asking questions. They were demanding answers.

Doc Savage faced Selan and the six advisors. He repeated the demands of the chiefs.

"King Udu will—oho-ho-ho-ho!" shouted the wrinkled Selan.

He and the others seemed convulsed with mirth. They howled until tears ran down their cheeks. They slapped each other's bared shoulders.

"Ho-ho-ho! Ho-ho! Ho-ho!"

Amazed chiefs arose. They brandished their spears and shouted.

This was a proclamation of war they could understand. They saw Selan and King Udu's advisors well pleased. From the appearance of the man of bronze and the silver casket bearing the body of Prince Zaban had come a strange inspiration.

The chiefs understood Selan, the great medicine man, to be well pleased. All of his glum expression was gone. Before the tribesmen, the seven representatives of King Udu continued to howl with laughter.

The chiefs rushed into the streets. The beat of the drums took on a fury of action. Each tribal chief called to his warriors. Hundreds of gleaming, oiled bodies started writhing in the weird dances that would arouse to killing fury.

Doc Savage did not delay. King Udu still was resting. The will to fight was not enough. The primitive warriors must have more expert direction.

The man of bronze hastened to present the names of Monk and Ham as officers who could help organize and lead the army of Kokoland.

Selan and the six advisors were still laughing. But they were becoming more subdued. Something strange had happened to them.

"These strange ones of Doc Savage then will be named to lead," agreed Selan, the medicine man. "The one called Monk, he is the greatest, so he shall be a chief. The other one, Ham, is smaller and of not so much presence. He will be made the leader of the carriers."

The six advisors agreed to these strange commissions for Monk and Ham. None quite knew to what Kokoland had been committed. The advisors who would have sacrificed the kingdom, through fear or their belief in the power of the Long Juju, would have slight headaches after it was all over.

The whipped cream Doc Savage had served on the white ant pie was a common mixture. The goat's cream had been shaken up with nitrous oxide under pressure. Its most common name is laughing gas. Once it was used by dentists.

Selan, the great medicine man, had laughed the loyal, primitive people of King Udu into a war of defense against all enemies.

Chapter XIV

RAID OF THE SHIMBA

UNDER strong stimulants, King Udu appeared before his palace. His vast, *chamma*-clad figure brought howls of approval. In the streets, the tribal chiefs were organizing their straggling, primitive warriors in their own manner.

Doc Savage realized even the inspiration of King Udu's appearance could not create an army to resist the modern weapons of the Asiatic and European adventurers beyond Mount Kibo. King Udu was using the last of his waning strength to come before his palace.

Thousands of barefooted followers jammed this royal avenue. It was a street thick with dust. This drifted like mist over the long, thatched hut, in which dwelt the Kokonese women.

"Either we get out of here and get some air, or we'll choke to death," declared Pat Savage to Señorita Moncarid.

"They do not permit the women to walk abroad when the war drums are being beaten," said Señorita Moncarid.

"Huh!" snapped Pat Savage. "Any time I need a permit to get my breath, I'll let your king know about it! Come on! The wind is blowing across the river! I'm half strangled!"

Señorita Moncarid reluctantly followed the impetuous Pat Savage. It was cooler and there was less dust by the river. Count Cardoti was walking toward the long hut of the women.

Perhaps he had arranged for Pat Savage and Señorita Moncarid to have better quarters.

Count Cardoti saw the figures of the two women vanish in the green bushes close to the slowly flowing stream, below the place of one of the war dances. The warriors from this dance now were thronging toward the king's palace.

Count Cardoti cried out, "Look out, Miss Savage! Señorita!"

As he called, Count Cardoti ran toward the river. Four long canoes glided into the quiet pool below the village.

Erect in the middle of one of these canoes, stood what at first appeared to be a shaggy animal. It was a man. But his body was wrapped in the tawny skin of a great male lion. The mane and the head of the beast concealed his features.

The man shouted in Masai.

"Seize them quickly! Also, get that other!"

From the bottom of the canoe heaved a bulky form. The unshaved face could hardly have been recognized. But Pat Savage identified the roaring voice of Renny.

"Back, Pat! They'll grab yuh! Holy——"

A knobby club slashed downward. Renny's thick skull took the impact of the blow. As he fell, Pat Savage heard the slapping of chains. She saw that Renny had been manacled to one of the cross-pieces of the long canoe.

"Renny! Renny! Doc's here!" cried Pat. "I'll——"

The brutal club struck again. Pat cried out in furious anger.

Señorita Moncarid caught at Pat's arm. But she was not quick enough. Pat had taken an automatic pistol from the bosom of her dress. The little weapon crackled viciously. In the long canoe, the first of the four warrior-filled craft, the oiled native who had swung the club, yelled in agony.

The club flew from the warrior's hands. Blood spouted from one of his arms. He splashed over the side into the river. Pat did not know why this warrior sank and did not arise. She knew nothing of the vicious, man-eating fish with the globular, staring eyes.

"Look out, Miss Savage!" Count Cardoti repeated, still running toward the river. Apparently he had no weapon.

Back of Count Cardoti some tribal warrior cried out loudly.

"The Shimba! The Shimba! *Ifehe! Ifehe!*"

No doubt the mysterious Shimba had struck great terror among some of the loyal tribes of King Udu. For the nearest group of warriors seemed to forget the purpose for which they held spears. Some cast their weapons aside. They dashed into the cover of the green liana wall of the jungle.

A few hardy tribesmen did not flee. This handful darted for the cover of a jutting point where the canoes must pass. This was a great mistake. The white man called The Shimba doubtless had planned this sudden descent very carefully.

Howls of pain broke out from the few warriors who had started throwing their long spears at the canoes. The liana wall seemed to come suddenly alive with small, thrusting tubes. Little darts made no sound.

The defending natives scattered as they fell. Some had been hit by as many as a dozen of the deadly barbs. One dart would have been sufficient.

"Back this way!" cried Señorita Moncarid to Pat Savage.

But Pat, heedless of danger, was running along the shore of the river. She was trying to follow the canoe in which she had seen Renny. She succeeded only in running directly into the jungle wall, through which the many, deadly blowpipes had appeared.

Señorita Moncarid followed. A strange thing happened. Pat Savage was seized and her cries were throttled by a pair of hands. The men holding Pat had hideously looped ears. They lifted their hands above their heads when Señorita Moncarid appeared.

"The Shimba! The Shimba!" they cried out.

It would be difficult to determine what they meant by that.

Señorita Moncarid did not retreat. Nor was she seized. It must have been she had decided to stick by Pat Savage.

Directly behind Señorita Moncarid came Count Cardoti. He was shouting angry words in Masai. The hands of two loop-eared warriors pinned his arms.

One of the laden canoes sheered close to the river shore. Pat Savage found herself lying on the bottom of this canoe. Near her, sat the rigid figure of Señorita Moncarid. The woman's lips were moving.

Pat could not read what she was saying. Señorita Moncarid was talking in the Masai tongue. Count Cardoti had been pushed forward toward the prow of the canoe.

A sharp order was rapped out by The Shimba in the lion's

pelt. The Masai warriors bent to their paddles. At the first turning, the four canoes glided into one of the narrow channels. Scores of these tortuous passages penetrated the jungle bush.

IN the meantime, Ham and Monk had been seeking Pat. A native had directed them toward the river. They arrived at the spot where the women had been seized. They had been close enough to hear screams.

"Howlin' calamities!" yelled out Monk. "It couldn't have been anybody but Pat! Look, Ham, here's her pistol! These other footprints are those of Señorita Moncarid!"

"I didn't trust that dame from the beginning!" barked Ham. "We can't get through this way without canoes! Come on! I'm sure they got Count Cardoti along with the others!"

Monk and Ham reached the place where Kokonese warriors had been wiped out by the poisoned blowpipe darts. The canoes had vanished.

After fighting their way a few yards through the liana vines, Monk and Ham discovered themselves helpless to follow farther.

King Udu's tribesmen were scurrying about in great disorder. The cry of "Shimba" had created widespread terror. Monk and Ham hastened to their bronze leader.

"We will not add to Pat's safety by hasty pursuit," said Doc Savage, when Monk and Ham sputtered out their story. "No doubt it is intended to create disorder. The one they call The Shimba is working with the invaders."

This was plain common sense. King Udu's tribesmen were scattered. For a time they seemed to forget they had a war on their hands. Logo, the man from far-away Long Island, became valuable in rallying the Kokonese. These in turn subdued some of the panic of the tribes from the hills.

"War or no war, we've gotta find Pat!" insisted Monk.

"War or no war, we will find her," agreed Doc. "She is safer for the time if we wait."

This seemed incredible to the impatient Monk. The ugly chemist had always been infatuated with the beautiful Pat.

King Udu's radio box was crackling. Doc apparently had expected this. The disturbance was in the short wave area.

"Renny's transmitter," said Ham. "We'll not get anything over that thing."

Ham was mistaken. A man's speech came in disconnectedly. But it was not Renny sending the message.

"DOC SAVAGE—"

This was repeated several times. The bronze man had no means of replying. He could only wait.

"The Shimba is speaking. We will keep the white woman and Colonel Renwick until you leave Kokoland—you have twelve hours—unless you are gone—the Masai woman remains with us—the other white man—twelve hours—"

The broadcast came in stuttering spasms. Many words were lost.

"It is as I thought," announced Doc. "I believe Pat and Renny will be held as hostages to insure our departure. Then they will be freed. I have no doubt the one called The Shimba has conspired to bring about the invasion. Certainly, he will want to avoid too many complications."

"I don't like it," said the stubborn Monk. "I'm for going into the bush and blastin' this Shimba off the map."

"We might blow up a thousand square miles of jungle swamp and never touch him," declared Ham. "But if we try to stop this army coming through the mountain pass, they'll probably torture Pat and Renny."

Doc Savage said nothing. He went into King Udu's royal bedroom. When he emerged, he was carrying a small canvas sack.

Monk gaped at him. Ham muttered under his breath. There were times when his closest companions did not quite understand the man of bronze.

Doc tossed the canvas bag into the cockpit of the shaky old Spad.

"We will get the plane into the open," he announced. "The fate of the whole kingdom and probably the security of Pat and Renny now rests on unexpected action. We must strike the first blow."

"Strike a blow with that wreck?" exploded Monk. "It won't even fly!"

The old Spad had been gassed. Its motor vibrated like a man with swamp ague. The canvas covered wings threatened to fall apart.

"Monk, the council has placed you in command of the Kokonese army," advised Doc. "Logo will be your aide. He will help you get the tribesmen together. Ham will look after the transportation. Move all available warriors at once toward the mountain pass of the Kilimanjaro."

"You mean—you don't mean I'm to be general of all these heathen?" spouted Monk, with his small eyes suddenly upon Ham. "An' the shyster here is only one of the boys that carries things?"

"King Udu's advisors have so decreed," said Doc. "Logo will help assemble the army. Collect all the blowpipes among the warriors."

With a rattling roar that threatened to tear it to pieces, the old Spad rolled down the open square in the village. Only a flying wizard could have contrived to lift the rickety plane's tail and not have nosed it over.

Monk took one look at the disgusted features of Ham.

"Well, sergeant!" snapped the chemist, suddenly elevated to the status of a general. "Take off your shoes! None of the carriers for this army wears em! We're marchin' barefooted!"

AIRMEN of the invading treasure hunters must have grinned among themselves. Their own trim pursuit planes lay in position for a dashing take-off. Their bombers were loaded with enough explosive to have blasted King Udu's village from the map.

"By all the saints!" grunted a flying captain. "Is that lunatic trying to conduct a lone raid or is he only spying on us quietly?"

The amused captain and his airmen smiled some more. Over the mountain range flopped and banged this vehicle of the air. If it had a greater ceiling, the flier was not attempting to use it. Perhaps he feared his bucking craft would fall to pieces if he ascended above two hundred feet.

"Doesn't seem much use to go up after him," smiled the amused captain. "Let him alone and he'll fall down himself."

It seemed as if this might happen. The airmen on the ground could almost see the whites of the flier's eyes. A dark face was stuck over the edge of the quivering cockpit of the Spad.

Plainly, this scout from Kokoland had come to look things over. So he was staying close enough to have counted the shining buttons on the airmen's uniforms.

Doc had wisely visited the *Wing* before making this aërial

dash over the mountains. The limited tank of the rattling old Spad carried only sufficient fuel for a couple of hours.

Johnny was sticking by the concealed *Wing*. The scholarly fellow would have been disgusted, had he not made a discovery. He had been bursting with his news.

"I've been getting a line on what all this war's about," Johnny told Doc. "The whole answer lies under the mountain."

But few men in the world exceeded Johnny in his knowledge of mineralogy. The man of bronze smiled at the discovery. But all of that could wait.

Johnny had seen two scout planes of the invaders flying high up. They had not detected the *Wing* hidden in the gorge.

"I believe they are planning to make an aërial attack within a few hours," was Johnny's belief.

"If something doesn't happen to upset their plans," stated Doc.

The amused captain of the airmen would not have believed the crippled old Spad could have affected his plans in the least. It did not seem as if the trembling wings of the ancient bus would ever carry it back over the mountains.

The Spad flew in circles. The dumb looking flier kept peering over the edge of the cockpit. Shooting him down wouldn't have been even good hunting.

Doc Savage pulled the Spad for a little more altitude. He tossed over a small round object. Apparently his aim was very bad. The object was a grenade. It caused a mushroom explosion not far from the line of pursuit ships. But it damaged nothing.

"We will have to send up a ship for him, after all!" said the captain. "One will be sufficient! If you fly close enough, the slipstream probably will knock him out of the sky!"

A pursuit plane screamed in a zooming take-off. The extremely modern war plane carried a gunner. Its machine gun snouts were so mounted as to sweep all of the area around the ship.

Doc was pulling the stick of the old Spad into his stomach. He was taking on more altitude. It seemed as if he were trying to escape the war hawk that flashed right onto his tail.

The gunner of the pursuit plane slapped a preliminary burst from both of his guns. The Spad trembled, fell off. It looked as if the smoke of the tracer bullets was about all the Spad needed to pull it out of the sky.

The legion airmen down below suspected the scouting flier was badly scared. Just when the Spad was in direct line of fire, its rickety wings tumbled into a spin. The old ship went around so fast it seemed it would screw its nose into the ground.

The pursuit plane was pulled up and leveled off. Little use to waste bullets on the obsolete native craft. By some miracle, the Spad missed a round hilltop. It slid out of sight of the airmen at the squadron camp.

"Crashed and he wasn't even hit," smiled the captain. "Well—"

He ceased speaking. He had been mistaken. Like a crippled bird, the Spad was beating its wings back into the sky. Doc was still flying low. His hands manipulated the stick as he played ski-jack with a few jutting shoulders of the hills.

The pursuit plane banked and waited. The Spad held too close to the ground to make power diving safe.

Suddenly the Spad seemed to have begun exploding on a new motor. Its wings must have been almost torn off. Doc sent it into a zoom that carried it five hundred feet above the pursuit plane.

The pursuit ship gunner let go one of his blasts. But the Spad flopped around. It could have been nothing but an accident that carried it just a few yards beyond the range of the screaming slugs.

Officers of the grounded squadron climbed a low hill above their camp, to watch the strange antics of King Udu's crazy scout plane. All of the squadron airmen streamed up the hill.

Doc again had jumped the old Spad out of a burst of machine gunfire. Unbelievably, he was flying upside down for several seconds.

"That heathen's either crazy or he's been imported from the United States," commented the captain. "None of the Kokonese ever learned to fly like that. They will bring him down on the reverse."

But the pursuit fliers did not bring the Spad down on the reverse. The amazing flier proved he knew all about an Immelmann.

Doc made no effort to use the machine gun of the Spad. It would have been impossible. Tropical rust had ruined the mechanism. Having been synchronized to shoot through the propeller, the gun now probably would have shot off the blades.

PERHAPS the legion fliers did not realize they were being drawn well away from their camp. Their lines of pursuit planes and bombers were now nearly half a mile back over a rolling hill.

Each second promised to be the last for the acrobatic old Spad.

"There's beginning to be something decidedly fishy about this," commented the captain. "No dumb sky pusher could have that many lucky accidents."

Doc Savage now was proving to the pursuit airman that even a crazy old Spad cannot be hit if properly handled. The pursuit ship was of the latest type. But it neither rolled nor winged over fast enough to trap King Udu's wandering scout.

More than two hundred officers and men of the flight squadron were grouped on the slope of a hill. The Spad was less than half a mile away. It was holding now at about five hundred feet.

Abruptly, Doc Savage was sliding the Spad toward the sloping hill. The power dive toward the ground group threatened to tear loose the plane's propeller. Some of the men on the ground yelled. They started running.

Doc Savage was peering down. The Spad was no more than fifty feet from crashing when its nose lifted. One bronze hand swept over the edge of the cockpit.

The pursuit plane screamed on the tail of the Spad. A stream of bullets chewed off the end of a wing. But the gunner was compelled to hold off his fire to avoid hitting his companions below.

Suddenly the fliers of the legion felt something like crystal snow stinging their cheeks. But when the flakes struck, they burst with a moist feeling on the skin.

The first of the running men fell down. They dropped so suddenly that their bodies flopped and plowed on down the hill.

The captain attempted to shout. Some of the flaky, crystal snow entered his mouth. His jaws remained wide open. He went to sleep on his feet and sat down.

The man of bronze was pulling the old Spad out of its wild dive. The fliers in the pursuit plane undoubtedly were swearing wildly.

Not one of their companions below remained on his feet. They lay all over the slope of the hillside, as if they had decided to take a midmorning nap. They had been due to move in an aërial raid over King Udu's kingdom at noon.

THE Spad did not zoom for great height now. It was being readily overtaken by the pursuit ship. The flier at the controls should have been more suspicious. Perhaps he did not notice the spreading clouds of blue mist which suddenly appeared ahead.

These little clouds had spread from a few small grenades tossed out by Doc. The motor of the pursuit plane sputtered. It did not pick up. All of its cylinders quit at once.

The pursuing gunner cursed wildly. He let go with both guns. But the nose of the pursuit ship had dipped. Contrary winds swirled over the Kilimanjaro. They caught the pursuit plane. It was being pulled down toward the pitted terrain, where the earth looked as if it were pockmarked by small volcanic craters.

Doc watched as the plane made a crippled landing. The blue mist had been a gas which was sucked into the motor of the other plane. It had congealed the fuel. Its effect was to so coat the cylinders as to make it necessary to take the motor apart, before it would function again.

The pursuit fliers would be hours getting back to the camp. Their companions would sleep all day from the effect of the anæsthetic.

Doc held the trembling Spad in a spiral bank above the trim lines of the grounded planes. Pursuit ships and bombers, they were all ready to blast King Udu's village.

The bronze man smiled grimly. He wiped some black smudge from his cheeks. Not a sign of life appeared in the squadron camp. Officers, airmen, mechanics and grease monkeys; all were sleeping beyond the hill.

The camp was in a safe spot. It had been deserted to watch the good show of a dumb, black aviator pitting a decrepit World War plane against a modern ship.

Doc pulled the Spad to a safe height. Small, glistening objects gleamed in the sun. A dozen of these fell among the modern planes of the European Legion.

The old Spad was being pulled toward Mount Kibo when

the first object exploded. A dozen blasts shook the mountain with terrific detonations. Where the invading squadron had been, was what looked like a new volcanic crater.

Chapter XV

THE BAREFOOTED ARMY

WITHIN the hour of Doc Savage's amazing attack upon the camp of the treasure-seeking invaders, a strange army moved.

Jungle animals on the rising slopes of Mount Kibo were silent. But in one spot a great howl was going up. This came from a human. He didn't resemble a man any too much. A great deal less did he resemble the one-time Brigadier General Theodore Marley Brooks, otherwise known as Ham.

It hardly seemed that this scrawny, barefooted object, ludicrously clad in a worm-eaten leopard hide, part of a Colobus monkey's fur and a few straggling ostrich feathers, could be the fashion plate of distant Park Avenue. Now and then he sat down abruptly. This was to extract thorns from his bare feet.

"Keep them carriers comin' along with the waterbags, sergeant!" piped up a childish voice. "The fellows up ahead are gettin' dry!"

"I don't care if you think you're sixteen generals, the next time you yelp at me I'm goin' to plug you with one of these blowpipes!" rapped out Ham. "Wait'll I find out how you managed to steal my clothes!"

Monk's only reply was an ugly leer. It hardly seemed possible the apelike chemist could have made his face any more homely, but he had.

"Brigadier General Andrew Blodgett Mayfair to you, sergeant," he grinned at Ham. "An' when we make camp to-night, I want you to help some of your boys wash my pig!"

Ham reared up suddenly. He waved a short, stabbing spear in his hand.

"I'll show yuh—" he yelled.

Monk ducked his head. But he need not have taken the trouble. Ham stepped on another thorn. The spear fell from his hand and he flopped on his knees.

A dozen Kokonese carrier-boys looked at the two men without expression. The army of King Udu was on the move up the mountainous Kilimanjaro jungle plateau.

Logo, the native from Long Island, had donned native garb. He was a stalwart warrior.

"My people believe you're some kind of a god," he told Monk on the side, as the nondescript army straggled from King Udu's village.

Logo had a sense of humor. He might have added he had heard the warriors say they believed Monk to be a god of the baboons. Many of the tribes worshiped the humanlike monkeys.

"I'll show them what a real general is like," boasted Monk. "I'll become one of them."

This was not difficult. Monk had shucked his clothes. His grotesque, hairy body, with the long trailing arms and the short legs, hardly needed the buffalo hide he had chosen to wrap around him.

This was a barefooted army. So Monk displayed his own huge feet. Though Ham was only a carrier sergeant, he would have disobeyed the order to lay aside his somewhat tattered raiment, which had been elegant enough when he had arrived.

Monk had taken care of that angle. Ham's clothes had been stolen. The lawyer could wear monkey fur and ostrich feathers or nothing.

"The tribal chiefs will obey your orders as long as you keep them believing you have superior knowledge," the astute Logo advised Monk.

So, at the first waterhole, the gorilla-like Brigadier General Monk suddenly appeared among the waterboys. The carriers were already kneeling to fill the waterbags of goat skin.

"Hold everything!" squeaked Monk. "None must drink of the water that burns!"

MONK truly was an appalling figure. He swung to the branch of a tree over the waterhole. Logo looked on with a wide grin. Monk wrapped one arm around the branch and looked into the pool.

"You never looked more natural!" rasped the disgusted and half naked Ham. "I hope you see your own face in that hole and it scares you to death!"

Monk's fingers appeared to touch the surface of the small waterhole. Instantly the black boys cried out and shrank away. Across the pool swept a blue flame. It spread until all of the water in the pool seemed to be blazing.

"See," announced Logo, "the fire of water does not burn one who is a god."

Monk apparently was bathing his naked feet in the blue fire. The carriers fled back into the jungle.

"If you think monkeyshines like that will lick an army, you're crazier than I always thought you were!" rapped Ham sarcastically.

Monk climbed from the tree. It would be many months before water would be taken from this pool by the natives. Monk stuck the vial of simple chemical he had employed back into his furs.

"That makes Monk a greater general than the licking of a dozen armies," advised Logo. "His orders will be obeyed."

It was a strange army moving up the mountain. Only King Udu's Kokonese had a semblance of order. Hundreds of wilder tribesmen filtered through the jungle armed only with their spears, blowpipes and oxhide shields.

Monk pranced about, as if he were not in the least aware he was leading this primitive horde to meet a modern army at the mountain pass, a few miles above. The natives were no more than an unorganized mob. They were on the way to battle the most modern war tanks, machine guns, high explosives and poison gas.

"With you reverting to what you've always been destined to be, this is nothing less than plain suicide," predicted Ham darkly.

"Anyway, we're safer here than back in the village if they happen to pull a sudden air raid," said Monk seriously. "I'm glad we got the army started before they found out King Udu seems to be dying."

MONK and Ham did not know then what had happened to the aërial squadron of the invaders. They were obeying certain instructions issued by their bronze chief.

While only some of the tribesmen were armed with their long spears, the primitive army carried all of the hundreds of blowpipes which could be gathered. It looked as if Doc Savage had decided to lay aside, for the time, his reluctance to be responsible for killing.

At this time, the old Spad was sputtering back over King Udu's village. The few old men and boys, and the women in the town must have been amazed to see the rickety bus return.

Selan, the medicine man, and the six advisors to the king, looked at Doc Savage with glittering eyes.

"King Udu believes we should send the women and the children into the hills to save them from the death from the air, which soon will come," announced the wrinkled Selan. "The king thinks his own hours are numbered. He wishes to remain here beside the body of his son."

"The women and children may remain in the village with safety," Doc stated. "The fliers of the devils beyond the mountains are taking a noonday sleep. They will awaken to find their planes have all been destroyed."

The man of bronze glided into the room where King Udu lay on the royal couch. He had not stated that though the aërial squadron had been wiped out, not a single man had been killed or even wounded.

Selan, the medicine man, would not have believed in such magic.

In the streets of the village, the drums were *tunk-tunking* ominously. The word had been passed out that King Udu was dying. Wails of women filled the thatched huts. Old men mumbled.

The hard heels of the hands pounding the drums were accomplishing what might amount to disaster.

Through the jungle, in the direction of Mount Kibo, other drums were being beaten. The tom-toms thumped from one hill, to another.

They were saying, "King Udu is dying! King Udu is dying! There is no hope! There is no hope!"

UNTIL this time the hundreds of Kokonese and tribesmen had been moving steadily forward through the jungle. Monk and Ham had been abusing each other with great fervor. As long as he lived, Ham would be remembering and seeking to repay the ugly chemist for this barefooted torture.

The primitive army had been moving silently, steadily. *Tunk-tunk* went the drums. Monk and Ham could almost feel the movement through the jungle coming to a pause.

Carrier boys suddenly laid down their goat skins of water. Some slashed the skins with their knives and permitted the fluid to run out on the ground.

"Logo, what do you think they're doin'?" yelled Monk.

The loyal black Logo shook his head sadly.

"They have been told the life blood of King Udu is ebbing," he sated. "If King Udu dies, all of the army will turn back. They will take it as an omen of disaster."

Monk loped back and forth through the jungle. A dozen feathered chiefs sat down stubbornly, waiting. They shook their heads when Monk attempted to get the army moving again.

Monk at last was forced to appeal to Ham.

"Listen, shyster, you've been a general," said Monk. "An' what does a general do when his army sits down on him?"

Ham grinned ironically. He forgot even the pain of his scratched feet.

"A good general stays behind an' gives his army a kick in the pants," he advised with a long face. "I don't know what a general does when his army isn't wearin' any pants."

Abruptly there came a change in the note of the drums. The beat was more rapid. The strokes set millions of brilliant birds chattering and squawking in the trees.

"*Ho-hee! Ho-hee!*" shouted the nearest tribal chiefs.

They leaped to their feet, chanting. They swung their great oxhide shields over their arms. Their long spears waved commands to their own people.

"*Ho-hee! Ho-hee! Ho-hee!*"

The cry became a steady chant around the mountain. It passed through the hundreds of the army. Once more the primitive horde of King Udu swept toward the mountain pass where modern weapons might soon annihilate them as easily as if they were so many flies.

Doc Savage sat beside old King Udu in the royal chamber—at the time the army moved again.

The access of strength which had brought King Udu before his advisors and his people was swiftly fading. It had been this new appearance immediately after Doc Savage's return that had started the drums beating the glad news; that had sent the primitive, barefooted army of tribesmen on toward the mountain pass.

The man of bronze had resorted to the most powerful stimulant. But King Udu was nearly one hundred years old. His great, fat body was already breaking up. Only the spirit that had hoped to save his people and his kingdom had kept King Udu living until this time.

When Doc emerged from the royal chamber, he held up his hand for silence. Selan's keen, black eyes glowed in his wrinkled face. The ancient medicine man was not to be greatly fooled.

Doc realized Selan and the other advisors would quickly turn to a rule of the Long Juju, where their supposed witchcraft would give them power. The man of bronze was worried over the captivity of Renny and Pat Savage, of Count Cardoti and Señorita Moncarid.

Upon the wrong move now would hang their lives.

The weird, fantastic army led by Monk and Ham and Logo, must remain at the mountain pass. Moreover, its primitive weapons must be made to prevail against the most efficient death-dealing machinery.

"The time has come to have the advice of great wisdom," said Doc solemnly. "Selan, it is with your eyes we must see the army which lies beyond the mountain. Their birds of death have been destroyed. You will come with me in the *Wing* that flies."

Selan, the man of great medicine, was susceptible to flattery. No doubt he realized the greatness of Doc Savage. Yet in his conceit, he forgot that his own belief in himself might be used against him.

"I will gladly accompany the great one, Doc Savage," bowed Selan, as if conferring a real favor. "I would have the experience of flying in the *Wing*."

Doc was using a radio transmitter. He contacted the short wave in the *Wing*. Johnny replied.

"Bring the *Wing* at once to the village of King Udu," directed Doc. "The wise one, Selan, who has great medicine, will observe with us the army of the invading devils."

Doc Savage knew this ruse must succeed. For on his royal couch of skins, King Udu was more than sleeping.

The king of Kokoland was dead. The army, his people must not know.

Chapter XVI

THE BURNING "WING"

MONK was informed of Doc Savage's summoning of the *Wing* to King Udu's village. Tropical darkness had struck across Mount Kibo. Scouts of the invading adventurers no doubt had reported the motley, barefooted army—a veritable primitive horde.

Commanding officers of the foot soldiers, the tanks and the light artillery, were preparing to move. Dazed, recovering airmen of the sky division were disbelieved.

It was difficult for officers of this great legion to accept such a story. That a disreputable old Spad of the World War period, flown by a lone lunatic, had wiped out a pursuit and bombing squadron.

Officers and fliers of the squadron found themselves disgraced. Orders were rapped out. Communication had been established with allied cohorts in the jungles. The Masai and Swahili, commanded by The Shimba, were ready to join in a quick invasion.

It was fantastic that the aërial squadron could not be sent ahead to bomb King Udu's kingdom and pave the way for the army.

But the army must move.

At this time, it might have been expected that King Udu's skin-clad, barefooted army would be mustering the few modern guns it had. Yet, except for the odd-looking superfiring pistols possessed by Monk and Ham, and one in the hands of Logo, no modern weapons were being prepared.

Any smart war correspondent would have been convinced Doc's companions were crazy. Judged by appearances, Monk and Ham would have been candidates for an asylum.

Monk's furry, red-haired body was crudely daubed with red and white ochre. Red-dyed ostrich plumes waving over his low forehead, gave him the appearance of some gorilla looking through a bush.

"If I can only live to remember what you looked like when they made you a general," grinned Ham. "We don't need any guns, ape. All you've gotta do is show yourself to the attacking army."

Monk, for once, was amiable. Ham himself was also striped with red and white ochre. One long ostrich feather drooped over his thin nose.

"If I can take your picture back to Park Avenue, that's all I ask," said Monk. "Especially when you were kickin' them boys around at the last waterhole."

"Confound your baboon brain, you didn't take any pictures, did you?" rapped Ham.

"It'll be a sensation, all right," grunted Monk.

HUNDREDS of tribesmen were lurking in the crevices and gullies of the Mount Kibo pass. Warriors shivered in fireless caverns in the volcanic walls of the mountain gorge. The song of the stonechat birds and the crickety chattering of mountain rats did not warm their nearly naked bodies.

With great reluctance, the chiefs had given orders to lay aside their spears, their bows and arrows. They would have preferred putting on a few war dances with blazing wood. Thus, they would have laid themselves open to massacre before the modern guns of the army they were soon to face.

And in preparation for this modern army, Monk, Ham, Logo and some of the more intelligent chiefs were working fiercely. Their occupation was too fantastic for belief.

Against war tanks, machine guns and repeating rifles, perhaps bombs of poison gas, the natives were loading thousands of the blowpipes. Other weapons had been laid aside.

Monk, Ham and Logo were preparing the small darts. As fast as loaded, the blowpipes were passed along both sides of the mountain gorge. It now seemed as if Doc Savage, in this extremity, had abandoned all thought of sparing lives.

For the blowpipes, of all weapons, were the most deadly at short range. The poison used by the natives on the barbs instantly paralyzed the hearts of those who were struck.

In the midst of the occupation, a tribal runner came breathlessly into the cavern where Monk and Ham were directing the defense.

"The foreign devils are moving," he announced, falling on

his face. "The elephants without heads trumpet before them."

"He means the war tanks," stated Logo. "Have all the chiefs been placed?"

The report was interrupted by a sudden hissing. What appeared to be a great, triangular system of neon lights arose over the pass. Tribesmen fell on their faces. This was the first view they had been given of Doc Savage's flying *Wing*.

Monk and Ham had been informed by radio of part of what had taken place in King Udu's village. But the man of bronze had not trusted the truth to the air. He feared the news of King Udu's death might be picked up by The Shimba with Renny's radio box.

"Now what do you suppose Doc is trying to do?" squealed Monk.

"I would say he is anticipating the initial maneuvers of our enemies," drawled a slow voice at the mouth of the cavern. "Doc is merely ascending to observe."

Johnny had come up the side of the pass.

"I wonder why he has all the lights going?" said Ham. "Looks like he's inviting trouble."

"I have been informed that is the purpose of this peculiar demonstration," advised Johnny. "The invaders still have a pursuit plane which might be employed to carry bombs."

"Say, but won't that bring the army hotfooting into the pass?" asked Ham.

"Perhaps," said Johnny. "But Doc also is taking that wrinkled old buzzard of a medicine man, Selan, for a little ride."

"Selan is with him?" exclaimed Logo quickly, his eyes piercing Johnny's with the question. "Then there must be a purpose?"

"Doubtless there is," advised Johnny, "but I have not been informed of all of it."

THE *Wing* swung into the mists higher up. Its ascent suddenly was checked. Monk, Ham and the others heard the whooming of an airplane motor.

"That's the one pursuit plane Doc didn't put out of business this morning," stated Johnny. "I think that was a mistake."

The low hissing of the *Wing* was altogether lost in the increasing thunder of the pursuit ship. Doubtless it was manned by the same fliers who had been so successfully tricked by the obsolete Spad. If so, they were out to get revenge.

"There won't be anything to that scrap," said Monk confidently. "I'd like to see what happens when those fellows hit the projector rays. Doc'll stop them like nobody's business. They're going high."

The two aircraft were seeking altitude. Apparently Doc was doing some experimenting in the climbing ability of the pursuit ship.

"Maybe he's just taking them for a ride along with that old monkey, Selan," observed Ham. "Too bad it couldn't be a real fight, so the medicine man could rattle the spare teeth he's wearing."

The *Wing* and the plane again swung downward over the mountain pass. The tube lights of the *Wing* marked its passage in the mist. The beating of the pursuit plane's prop indicated it was close to the other craft.

Red fire blossomed like two pinwheels. This was accompanied by the chattering of machine guns.

"Might as well save their ammo," commented Ham. "I wonder if Doc will feed their motor some of the cold gas?"

The question was given an unexpected answer. Certainly it was not cold gas that suddenly expanded with the glare of a bursting sun over Mount Kibo and the pass.

All of the stark outlines of the volcanic mountain leaped into view. It was like the sun had suddenly been turned into the middle of the tropical night.

"Well, I'll be superamalgamated!" rapped Johnny. "The plane has smacked into the *Wing!* Our gas was not combustible! Now what's happened? Doc hasn't a chance!"

Monk and Ham gasped. They were too paralyzed to speak.

The *Wing* seemed to have fallen into thousands of small pieces. In the great flare of light, the pursuit plane of the legion was whisked upward as if driven by a hurricane wind. All of the air seemed to be sucked from the pass by the great explosion.

Among the echoes came the rattle and clatter of metal clanking on rocks. Some of the scared tribesmen called out. They were dashing away from a sloping side of the great gorge.

Parts of the *Wing* were falling like a rain of death.

"Doc!' Doc!" yelled Monk. "He didn't have time to jump!"

"He must have seen what was coming," insisted Ham. "He would not be caught in that kind of a trap. We'll find him somewhere close by. I'll bet he'd save old Selan, too."

AWE-STRICKEN natives avoided the spot where the flying *Wing* had been scattered. The metallic parts covered a space of several hundred yards. Monk led the scramble to the spot.

"Hey, Doc!" yelled the big chemist. "You all right?"

There was no answer. For a long distance, all of the rocks were bare. Johnny had caught up an infra-red beam projector. He clapped goggles like milk cans over his eyes. Monk and Ham jammed on their own infra-red observers.

"I would not make too much noise," advised the smart Logo suddenly. "We should not permit the tribesmen to discover what may have happened."

"Dag-gonit! Dag-gonit!" squawked Monk. "Nothin' could have happened to Doc!"

Johnny was not so sure. They had swept all of the possible space where a parachute might have descended.

"The down draft of night wind from the mountain would have carried a 'chute right into the pass," stated Johnny. "I fear we can arrive at only one conclusion."

Though they scoured the base of the mountain wall, no trace of the bronze man was found.

But near one of the caverns, Logo cried out.

"Selan! It's the medicine man!"

The wrinkled old medicine man was crouched in a niche of the wall.

"Where is his parachute?" demanded Ham. "What happened to Doc? Ask him, Logo. I don't get his crazy lingo."

Logo questioned old Selan. The medicine man shook his wrinkled jaws and mumbled.

"Selan says he was placed here to wait by Doc Savage," interpreted Logo. "He would not permit him to ascend to meet the enemy."

It was the steady, well balanced Johnny who assumed command. He led the sad group back to the cavern. From the distance came the rumbling of moving war tanks.

Chapter XVII

KING UDU'S RESURRECTION

KING UDU was dead. Selan, the ancient chief of medicine men, was absent. Thus the news was withheld for some time. But in the night, came a wailing chant from the king's palace.

The six remaining advisors were forced to come before the people. Before they did this, they saw that King Udu's body was prepared to lie in tribal state on the royal couch.

Chanters sat on the earthen floor. They rocked their bony bodies.

"*Ai-ee! Ai-ee! Ai-ee!*"

The strident wail reached the old men in the huts. It was carried on in the long hut of the women. Children awakened to join the tribal lament.

Tunk-tunk-tunk-tunk!

Once more the skin drums conveyed their message. Because of the explosion of Doc Savage's *Wing*, and the roaring of oncoming army tanks of the invaders, the telegraph tom-toms of the hills were slow in transmitting their message.

Monk showed unexpected genius. He was among the first to hear the slow dirge of the drums. This was because the apelike chemist still was searching the slopes where the man of bronze might have fallen.

"Dag-gonit! It couldn't have happened to Doc!"

Monk's ugly face worked with grief. He examined parts of the fallen *Wing*. The explosion had been terrific. Yet Monk knew the gas of the *Wing* itself was noncombustible. Some twisted metal containers had not been destroyed. Monk examined these.

A queer understanding light appeared in Monk's small eyes.

"I'll bet that's the answer," said the chemist. "That would have blown the old mountain itself to bits."

Not for nothing was Monk a great industrial chemist. He had discovered Doc had been carrying high explosive bombs.

Now he heard the death message of the drums. He had learned to read the *tunk-tunking* of the hollowed logs.

"So, that's what Doc was trying to cover up," muttered Monk. "He knew King Udu was dead, so he took the old medicine man away before he could start trouble."

MONK loped with ungainly strides back to the cavern. If the tribal chiefs scattered about the mountain pass got the message of the drums, it would send their warriors pell-mell in retreat.

Monk came leaping into the big cavern where Ham, Johnny, Logo, old Selan and a dozen of the tribal chiefs were gathered. He could tell they had not yet heard the message of the drums.

"Well, I'll be superamalgamated!" gasped Johnny. "He has been seized with anthropoidal psychosis!"

Ham looked at Monk with worried eyes. Logo showed that he thought Monk had gone crazy.

"*Ho-hee! Ho-hee! Ho-hee!*" yelled Monk.

His childlike voice was a shrill scream. Jumping across the cavern, Monk seized the sticks of one of the greater drums. This was an immense, hollowed *senecio* trunk with dried Kudu skin over its end.

"*Ho-hee!* Howlin' calamities! *Ho-hee!* Make ready!"

Bang! Bang! Bang! Bang!

Monk's powerful muscles rapped the stick across the skin drum. He was hitting twenty tremendous slow beats to the minute. It was like the tolling of a great muffled bell.

At the same time, Monk's lips were moving. He was looking at Ham and Johnny. They began to understand. All of Doc's men were expert lip readers. Monk was talking to his companions silently.

Logo and old Selan did not get it. Perhaps the wise Logo understood partly.

"King Udu is dead," Monk was saying with his lips. "We must cover up! Call the tribes to attack!"

His measured beating of the tom-tom was the tribal call to battle. Twenty slow beats to the minute. But they filled the pass. Some of the nearer tribesmen immediately took up the drumming.

Ham and Johnny acted. From the *Wing* had been brought boxes of supplies. Now hundreds of queer goggles were being passed through the chiefs to their warriors. Many viewed these with distrust.

"These will make your people see where there is no sight," was the advice from the smart Logo. "The coming devils will march in darkness, but they will appear in your eyes."

ONE of the assembled chiefs cast his goggles down. He showed every evidence of superstitious fear.

"Voodoo devils," he mumbled. "I hear a distant message."

Monk confronted the tall warrior. It was time for a demonstration. He fastened a gorillalike hold on the tall chief's wrist. The savage leader squirmed, but he was powerless. Monk was using one of the paralyzing grips taught by Doc Savage.

Below the cavern, the pass was a bowl of darkness. It was as thick as smoke. Monk pointed one hand at this.

"Johnny, the magic!" he rapped out.

Johnny understood. He picked up one of the infra-red beam projectors. The invisible light shot across the pass. Monk clapped the goggles on the helpless chief's eyes. He turned the savage around.

"Now you see where there is no sight!" announced Monk in the chief's own language. "All of your people will be greater than the Long Juju! We prepare to resist the invading devils!"

The chief saw clearly where there was no light. All of the pass showed in black and white. And he could pick out his own warriors crouching among the rocks.

"*Ho-hee! Ho-hee!*" cried the chief.

The other chiefs donned the goggles. They joined in the cry of battle. The banging of the battle drums still submerged the slower telegraph of the drums in the hills.

"See that all of the blowpipes are placed!" commanded Monk.

Ham seldom admitted Monk amounted to anything. Now the lean face of the lawyer held some admiration.

"Sometimes, you confounded insect, I think you've got brains," he said grudgingly.

Then he spoke quickly, in the language of the ancient Mayans.

"But if these heathen get wise the old king has passed out, we are sunk. With Doc gone and King Udu dead, these natives would quit on us cold."

Old Selan, the wrinkled medicine man, bored his black eyes into Ham. All this time, he had been sitting in dejected silence. Ham had made a great mistake.

The Mayan language was little known. Doc and his men employed it to confuse their enemies. But one man in the kingdom of Kokoland knew the Mayan language.

Old Selan understood what Ham had just said.

"*Ai-ee! Ai-ee! Ai-ee!*" the wrinkled medicine man suddenly screamed. "The white chief lies! King Udu is dead! The Long Juju will rule!"

Before he could be seized, the old medicine man had dashed from the cavern. Almost at once, a near-by drum changed its war beat.

The warrior chiefs in the cavern cast themselves on their faces. They joined in the wailing chant which old Selan had started.

"Now the devil and all's to pay!" rapped out Johnny, forgetting his long words. "That's what Doc was trying to keep under cover when he brought old Selan up here!"

"There's nothing we can do," said Logo. "All of the tribesmen and our own loyal Kokonese will quit cold. We are defeated by our own people before the battle begins."

As wailing panic spread among the hundreds of tribesmen in the mountain pass, the chanters mourned in the palace of King Udu. The death torches of nut oil were lighted. Before the great throne room, a dozen tom-toms tunked out the grief and despair of the stricken people.

In strange contrast, the loud strains of a jazzy band march broke in on the drums. The music was military. It sounded like some naval band. For a few moments it drowned out the dirge.

This weirdly unexpected music was coming from the old king's powerful, modern radio. It was indeed a naval band. And the band was playing a war march.

The radio stood across the royal throne from the hundreds of skulls of beheaded enemies. Before the doorway where King Udu lay, was piled an assortment of objects.

Those were the lifetime adornments and weapons of King Udu's family for generations. Vessels contained meats. A white goat was alive. He bleated shrilly. The Kokonese had prepared their stricken monarch for his journey into another land.

Oil torches gave dim light in the royal death chamber. The great bulk of King Udu lay on the couch of skins. In the same room still reposed the casket containing Prince Zaban.

Tom-toms beat. A radio gave forth the strains of a modern military march.

Skulls of the beheaded grinned down on the painted chanters. A dozen guards with long spears stood before the death chamber door.

All the tribal fetishes were represented in preparation for King Udu's death journey.

Old men ground their wrinkled foreheads in the dust of the streets and mumbled. Women wailed in the long hut.

The guards with the spears were standing as impassive as statues of carved mahogany. Their giant bodies were dyed vividly red.

At the edge of King Udu's village, the earth trembled. There arose a thunderous trumpeting that drowned both the radio band and the tom-toms. The Kokonese were bringing up the elephants.

The passing of the elephant herd was a funeral custom. Sometimes the mourners failed to move from before the elephants. Some would be trampled. But mostly the wise beasts stepped over them.

THE radio band crashed to a finish. From inside the palace came wild cries. First, the chanters came rushing into the street. They were followed closely by the guards. The guards flung away their spears and fled.

The six wrinkled medicine men, the advisors, were the last to emerge. They tried to conceal their terror. With upraised hands, they were invoking the gods in mumbling voices.

The immense figure of old King Udu came walking behind the advisors. On his tremendously fat body hung death ornaments. From his neck and arms and hands gleamed countless jewels. The tribal death mark was on King Udu's forehead.

The fat old body of the ruler of Kokoland quivered as he walked. But his eyes were black and keen beside the high-arched nose. His voice spoke clearly above his rolling chins.

"A great mistake has been made," he stated calmly. "I have only been sleeping. I have defeated the attempt of my enemies to put me to death. Bring the elephants, even the funeral herd. I shall go to lead my army."

The wrinkled advisors fell on their faces. Fat King Udu, very much alive, walked down the incline from his palace into the street.

ONLY an increased chirping of the stonechat birds, and a subdued chattering of hyrax, indicated the tropical dawn was not far away. Thick mists crowned Mount Kibo and all of the Kilimanjaro.

"Don't seem any use," groaned the voice of Monk. "Some of the chiefs are ordering their men to throw away the infra-red goggles."

"Yes," stated Logo. "They now believe they have been tricked. They are saying you are yourselves of this devil army and you have brought them into this pass to be killed. They are preparing to leave."

"I haven't heard the war tanks moving for some time," advised Johnny, who had been outside scouting along the wall of the gorge. "It doesn't look good. The invaders will wait until just before daylight to strike. A great many of the tribesmen are sneaking down the mountain."

"Dag-gonit!" groaned Monk. "I oughta choked that old medicine guy to death while I had him here! We've got to put up some kind of a fight! I'll go out and try and talk to them!"

Monk emerged on the rocks outside the cavern. He played a flashlight over his gorillalike figure, so he could be plainly seen. That was a mistake.

Excited tribesmen shouted. Bow strings twanged. A shower of arrows slapped about the mouth of the cavern.

"Ouch!" howled Monk. "The ornery heathen!"

An arrow stuck bloodily in his shoulder. Ham pulled him back into the cave. From the upper end of the pass came the explosion of war tanks' motors.

The invading army was starting its drive through the pass.

Chapter XVIII

THE ARMY STRIKES

THE horde of Monk's Kokonese and the allied tribesmen had begun their retreat. At the sound of the attacking movement, the terrorized natives scrambled back to the walls. The beat of the drums mourning the death of King Udu was suddenly stilled.

"If we only had some way to get them fighting mad," declared Ham. "The trouble is that old voodoo man, Selan, is hooked up with the Long Juju stuff. I wouldn't be surprised but what he has been playing in with The Shimba all the time."

"Thunderation!" exploded Monk. "That ain't the worst of it! I know now this Señorita Moncarid is running part of this unholy show! I wouldn't be surprised if she is The Shimba!"

Logo shook his head.

"I think you are mistaken," he asserted. "She is a prisoner along with your Miss Savage."

"That may be true," stated Ham, "but with Doc gone, it looks bad for all of us. If this army drives through, whoever The Shimba might be, Pat and Renny are done for."

In the pass below came the rustling of many bare feet. From the upper end of the pass a few guns crackled sharply. Apparently, the army leaders believed a few tribal guards had been placed at the pass.

The clanking of the war tanks and the movement of light artillery told plainly the invaders were moving in massed force. A few howls of death agony floated up to the cavern.

The retreat of the tribesmen had begun. It had become a rout.

"Howlin' calamities!" snapped out Monk. "This may be the finish, but I'm goin' to fight!"

Blood dripped from his shoulder where Johnny had extracted the arrow. The apelike chemist started to spring again into the open.

"*Kafee! Kafee!*" This meant, "Kill! Kill!"

This wild cry broke from the back of the cavern. Led by two hideously painted tribal chiefs, a dozen warriors burst into the rock room. They held long spears poised. These ringed in Monk and the others.

"*Kafee! Kafee!*" again cried one of these chiefs.

He shook his feathered head ornaments. From under one side, a great loop of flesh fell down onto his shoulder.

"Masai!" shouted Logo. "Selan and The Shimba have betrayed us even among our own people!"

Monk and Johnny had whipped out their superfiring pistols. The tribesmen had never seen these in action. They could not use their spears quickly enough. The pistols moaned. The two chiefs fell down. Some of the spearmen dropped their weapons.

But others were pouring into the cavern.

"Our only salvation is to surrender!" advised Logo. "We cannot overcome all of them!"

SUDDENLY the whole pass seemed to be split by a trumpet-like blast. More guns of the army were cracking. It was too dark to pick out targets. An occasional howl told of a hit.

With the trumpeting came a thunderous tramping below the cavern. A brilliant flare burst between the mountain walls. Into this almost blinding light appeared a single mass.

"Well, I'll be superamalgamated!" exclaimed Johnny. "It's an elephant, the biggest I ever saw!"

The beast was as big as a small house. His trunk stuck out rigidly. His trumpet blast was like the scream of a locomotive. His vast red mouth was a cavern of furious sound. Long tusks gleamed in the strange glare.

This white light was coming from the ground. It seemed to have burst from a dozen points. Hundreds of fleeing tribesmen fell upon their faces, groveling in the rocks.

"Great Julius Caesar!" rapped out Ham. "If it ain't old King Udu himself, in person!"

The immense, fat figure of King Udu sat upright on the head of the monster elephant. Rolls of copper and brass wires hung from his neck and arms. Weirdly cut jewels played from his hands and ears.

"Great Scott!" cried Logo, with a peculiarly American phrase. "He's wearing the funeral headdress! King Udu was dead, and he has come to life with all of his death ornaments!"

The strangely burning, chemical light played for perhaps less than half a minute. In these thirty seconds, King Udu raised one tremendous arm. His old voice rolled clear and strong.

"Turn back, my people!" he commanded. "My enemies have said I was dead! You see for yourselves, I live! I have come to command you! We will not yield our kingdom! You see what I bear!"

"Howlin' calamities!" yelled Monk. "The war's on again! Logo, can you make them dumb chiefs understand to do, as we planned?"

Logo was staring at the figure of King Udu.

"It's the Blood Idol!" he shouted. "The Blood Idol has come back to the kingdom! Look!"

Monk, Ham and Johnny could see only a great splash of scarlet in the middle of the fat King Udu's breast. This caught the white light and threw it back with flashes of blinding red. An enormous jewel of some sort hung by a chain around the ruler's neck.

PERHAPS the advance guard of the army was too surprised to act quickly. The white glare revealing King Udu and the mammoth elephant was dying before the first guns flamed. A machine gun chattered then from one of the clanking war tanks.

A trumpeting scream of death agony burst from the elephant. The huge pachyderm settled over on one side like a great house falling on the rocks. The fat King Udu rolled off.

At this instant, the flare of light from the ground winked out. The mountain pass was plunged into Stygian darkness.

But now the tribesmen of Kokoland were shouting the cries of war. King Udu lived.

Monk gave the word and Logo passed it along. The drums beat as had been ordered previously.

"I will try and get King Udu up here!" shouted Ham. "Perhaps the bullets did not hit him!"

As if in reply, came King Udu's clear, old voice in the darkness.

"I am unharmed, my people! I am with you as you fight!

Stop these invaders of the kingdom! I am your king! The Blood Idol speaks!"

It was well for the hundreds of loyal tribesmen they could not then see what was happening in the darkness.

The hundreds in the higher rocks were equipped with the infra-red goggles. Searchlights leaped out on the war tanks. Foot soldiers were marching in long files. But the lights did not find the hidden natives.

From the cavern, Monk and Johnny were operating two huge boxes which had been brought from the *Wing*. Generators hummed. Invisible to all but those with the goggles, fanlike beams played over the white army with its modern weapons.

Machine guns rattled from the tanks. Some of the soldiers were shooting with repeating rifles. Lead spattered aimlessly along the walls. The searchlights were of little value in picking out the hidden tribesmen.

"LET 'em have it!" yelled Monk. "Feed 'em the darts!"

Logo translated the command with a shout of his own.

King Udu had returned from the dead. Or, he never had been dead. Wild tribesmen, firm believers in witchcraft, found themselves looking through the glasses that could see in the darkness.

"*Kafee! Kafee!*" shouted many chiefs.

The war drums rolled in sudden clamor. Hemmed in the pass below, unable to pick out more than a few figures on the honeycombed walls, the foot soldiers of the invading army set themselves for a burst of gunfire.

None came. The soldiers themselves were in opaque darkness. It lacked only a few minutes to the tropical dawn. But these few minutes were sufficient.

The bony, scholarly Johnny was dancing up and down. He was looking through a pair of the huge goggles.

"Never but once in a lifetime could a man ever have opportunity to observe such a manifestation of psychological suggestion," stated the geologist.

Modern weapons were rattling their bullets into the air. The black warriors had laid aside their spears, their bows and arrows, their great oxhide shields and even the few antique guns they possessed. Those with the goggles, held blowpipes to their lips.

"By all the saints, the poisonous devils!" screamed a white officer in the army and fell on his face.

Others were falling down. Some were shooting, but they had no marks. Among the soldiers rained tiny darts. They were striking with uncanny accuracy. The barbs stuck in faces and necks. When they missed, they seemed to make mushy little explosions as they struck the rocks.

"Great guns!" squealed Monk. "Look! They think they're all being poisoned, Johnny!"

The white men of the invading army thought just that. They could see but little. They dropped like flies. Some screamed. They had heard much of the poisoned blowguns of these savages.

Drivers of the tractor tanks found themselves blocked. The bodies of the marching soldiers piled before them. They did not want to crush the dead.

These drivers and gunners would have been surprised to know there was not a dead man yet in the pass. The blow-pipe darts had been loaded with anæsthetic chemicals. The victims would sleep for perhaps a day, and they would feel rather groggy afterward.

"That just about puts a quietus on this invasion," stated Johnny.

"Dag-gonit! I told them not to use them spears!" said Monk.

Armed with the superfiring pistol, Monk slid down the wall. Some of the war-enthused tribesmen were hurling spears. A few were shooting arrows. These did not have goggles. Some soldiers now were being wounded and killed.

THE drivers and gunners of the tanks suddenly went to sleep. Their motors continued to hum, but the tanks did not move.

Tropical dawn was the usual blast of light. It revealed a mountain pass apparently choked with dead men. The invaders lay in grotesque heaps. Painted, whooping tribesmen were hard to restrain.

"I'll shoot alla you myself, if you start murderin' anybody!" yelled Monk.

The chemist did let go at one bloodthirsty band with his superfirer. This had the effect of quelling others. The hundreds of warriors now regarded Monk as no less than a real god. Even if he looked like only a god of the baboons.

Monk and Johnny climbed on the war tanks. Loaded with the weapons of the sleeping army, the warriors of Kokoland started triumphantly back toward the village of King Udu.

"Dag-gonit!" complained Monk. "Now what do you suppose became of Ham and the old king himself?"

"The Masai!" exclaimed Logo. "It is lucky this was all over before our people discovered it! The Shimba must have trailed King Udu! And they have seized the one you call Ham!"

"If it ain't one thing, it's a couple more!" howled Monk. "First, we lose Renny and Pat Savage! Then Doc disappears with the *Wing!* Now them black devils have grabbed Ham and the king himself!"

It seemed no doubt this was true. For three black warriors lay close to the dead elephant. Their ears showed the hideous loops of the Masai. Monk pointed out where their faces had been stuck with the drugged point of Ham's sword.

There must have been a tough, but brief battle. In the face of the battle, King Udu and Ham had been seized.

The hundreds of tribesmen were now too intoxicated with their amazing victory to show anxiety over the absence of King Udu. Perhaps each group imagined the king was with some other, or had returned to the village.

Logo hastily directed the concealment of the unconscious Masai. Luckily, the Kokonese showed some reluctance at approaching the slain pachyderm. The bull elephant was one of the funeral herd.

"I haven't seen old Selan, the medicine man, anywhere," stated Johnny. "I'll bet that wrinkled old buzzard had something to do with grabbing the king."

Logo was staring at the ear of the dead elephant. He gasped with amazement. Then he lifted the leathery flesh.

"Howlin' calamities!" squawked Monk. "The old king was pretty smart!"

An enormous red jewel had been hidden in the elephant's ear. It was a grotesque figure. It seemed to be partly a man and partly a scorpion.

"The Blood Idol!" said Logo. "We must get back to the village!"

Chapter XIX

THE BURNING KING

FOR the first time in the history of the village, modern war tanks ground and clanked through the dusty streets. The capital of Kokoland blazed with fires of victory.

Giant plumed warriors, glistening with oil, their faces made into many hideous masks, pranced and whooped after their own tribal customs. Stacks of modern rifles, machine guns and light pieces of artillery were packed into the great throne room of King Udu.

"Dag-goned if it don't seem to me them skulls are grinnin' more than they did before," pointed Monk. "We've won a war, an' what do we get out of it? Doc's gone. Pat and Renny and Ham maybe have been killed. Even King Udu comes back to life and they grab him. We've got to do something."

"If we had hold of that old buzzard, Selan, I'll bet we could get a line on where these Masai hold out," mused Johnny. "Logo, what do you think?"

"I've talked with Selan's medicine men, the advisors, and they know something they don't want to tell," said Logo. "But be prepared for action. I've still got a card up my sleeve."

In the streets, the tom-toms beat with wild fury.

The great elephant may have been one of the sacred funeral herd, but he was meat. Steaks of the pachyderm were being boiled. The feet were being baked in pits.

"I had some elephant steak once," said Johnny. "I boiled it from Monday morning until Friday night. Then I chewed it from Friday night until Monday morning. By that time I had enough elephant steak to last me the rest of my life."

Monk was not listening. He was watching Logo. Suddenly

the man from Long Island produced the red, flashing jewel taken from the ear of the elephant.

"The Blood Idol!" gasped the medicine men in unison.

All six fell on their faces. They mumbled in their native tongue. All seemed strangely stricken.

"These men of Doc Savage have saved the kingdom!" thundered Logo. "Now they must know more of The Shimba! That which Selan knew and concealed from his king, must now be told! The Blood Idol will strike death to those who evade the truth!"

The threat brought a few seconds of silence. Then all of the medicine men tried to talk at once. Neither Monk nor Johnny could make head or tail of their jabbering.

"I have it!" shouted Logo. "The white invaders have been left helpless! While the blood of the warriors is hot, we will strike again! They have told me the place of the Long Juju!"

SMOKY fires blazed on a flat, stone shrine or altar. This was a broad platform. On its top was a smaller table of stone. Around this flat stone walked two hideous figures. On the rough table a body lay under a white sheet. The two figures chanted.

One was a man. The other was a woman. The man was fantastically garbed in blood-red garments. His face was ochred to resemble a skull. The skull grinned at the woman.

The woman wore only a flowing robe of green. It was woven with many serpents. They had wings. They were the "Flying Green Serpents" of voodooism. The woman's face was fat and oily.

The man was the *Papa Loi*. The woman was the *Maman Loi*.

They were the priest and priestess of the Long Juju.

Old women stirred a filthy mixture of blood and goat's meat in a great pot. They stirred this boiling mess with their bared hands. The skin and flesh was all burned away.

Hideous warriors pranced slowly around a fire on the ground. In the horrible loops of their ears were many bright objects. Their long spears were brandished close to the faces of the prisoners chained to stakes driven into the ground.

"Holy cow!" groaned the deep voice of a heavily bearded man. "An' Doc got himself blown to pieces in the *Wing?* There ain't much hope for any of us then! If there was only some way to get Pat and the señorita outta this mess!"

Big Renny was so loaded with chains he looked like a statue of rusty iron. The chains were looped over a heavy stake.

Beside him another figure, more waspish, also was chained to a stake. This man spoke out of the corner of his mouth.

"Don't get too downhearted, Renny. We're not dead yet. You may get a big surprise."

Despite his position, the queerly clad Ham was grinning as if he knew something he could not divulge.

The enormously fat old King Udu was among the prisoners. His corpulent arms and legs had been loaded with chains. Only the stake behind him prevented the aged king from sagging to the ground.

Many jewels had been stripped from King Udu's body. There had been howls of rage when the Masai had discovered the Blood Idol to be missing. The raiding warriors, directed by the mysterious Shimba, had seen the king's display of the great, red gem.

But when King Udu and Ham were seized, the Blood Idol had vanished. After he had craftily placed the jewel fetish in the ear of the elephant, King Udu had appeared to lapse into a coma.

Perhaps the old king's apparent revival from death was only a flash. The tired heart must have been nearly exhausted under all of that mountain of flesh. And King Udu had not the satisfaction of knowing that his appearance had caused the defeat of the invading army.

King Udu's eyes were closed. His head with its straggling white locks was drooping. The arched nose was buried in his multiple chins.

Perhaps the old king realized he had saved his kingdom for the time. Perhaps he was only exhausted. He did not seem to know that the fierce Masai and Swahili warriors were being worked into frenzy for a new descent upon his village.

Papa Loi chanted. He walked up and down, keeping time with his hands to the slow beating of the skin drums. The eyes of all the Masai warriors were upon him.

The hideous face of the *Maman Loi* leered at the dancers. The old women mumbled and stirred the pot.

"WARRIORS of the Masai!" spoke a commanding voice. "The Long Juju demands the sacrifice of the white goat! With this Juju none of our enemies can survive!"

The speaker wore a strange combination of monkey fur and lion's pelt. His upper body was wholly concealed by the flowing mane of the lion and the enormous head. His voice came through the gleaming teeth of the man-eating beast.

He was The Shimba. Near him, another white man hovered in the background. This man seemed to have been wounded. His head was downcast.

"*Ho-hee! Ho-hee!*" chanted the warriors.

"Thunderation!" growled Renny. "That don't sound like the same Shimba that tried to drive me outta this heathen country! What in the devil does he mean by the white goat?"

The grin suddenly was erased from Ham's thin face.

"Renny, where's Pat, an' where that Señorita Moncarid?" he rapped out.

"I don't know where they've tied 'em up," stated Renny. "They took them away somewhere with that Count Cardoti fellow. They—"

Something was coming to a climax. The chanting of the *Papa Loi* became a frenzied outburst. The *Maman Loi* swayed and groaned.

Masai warriors slapped their spears into the ground. They howled like wild animals. Some were slashing their own bodies with sharp rocks. Blood lust apparently was being stirred.

On the stone platform, the *Papa Loi* dipped his hand into the mixture of goat's meat and blood. He held his dripping fingers to his lips. Then he let out a blood-curdling shriek.

"The white goat! The white goat!" thundered the voice of The Shimba. "It is the Long Juju!"

The hand of the *Papa Loi* swept away a cloth covering that had been over the small stone table. Renny heaved in his chains and roared. Ham strained and fought silently.

The *Papa Loi* whipped a long knife from his clothing. He threw up his hand.

Clad in a winding white sheet, her beautiful face as still as if she were sleeping quietly, Patricia Savage lay on the stone altar. This was the "white goat."

The *Papa Loi* whirled the knife. He swung and pranced.

"*Ai-ee! Ai-ee! Ai-ee!*"

THE Masai warriors had started screaming. But they had turned their eyes from the altar of the white goat. They were no longer looking at the *Papa Loi*. They did not hear the shouting voice of The Shimba.

All were looking at the enormously fat body of King Udu.

A terrible, an unbelievable thing was happening.

The vast, corpulent figure of the Kokoland ruler was dissolving. From his feet to his flowing white hair, King Udu seemed on fire. He was glowing with a weird, blue flame. The blaze seemed to crackle and consume his flesh.

"Seize him! It's a trick—it's—"

The Shimba was yelling. But his Masai warriors seemed turned to stone.

Not only was King Udu a blue pillar of fire, his flesh was apparently being rapidly consumed. Great rolls of fat were peeling off. Because of this, the many chains were clanking to the ground.

"Holy cow!" gasped Renny. "I might have known—"

Masai warriors were falling on their faces. Even the *Papa Loi* and the *Maman Loi* had ceased chanting. The *Papa Loi* stood as if frozen. The gleaming knife was still uplifted.

More than a hundred pounds of flesh rolled from the figure of old King Udu. Then the king was standing erect. From his still melting body issued the most fantastic sound the Masai had ever heard.

It was like the trilling of some death bird in a tomb. It was a weird warning. No doubt it struck a chill to the superstitious hearts.

"Doc! Doc!" shouted Renny. "Look out! He'll get Pat!"

The *Papa Loi* had whirled with his knife. But from the fat old body of what had seemed to be King Udu, sprang the amazing man of bronze.

Doc's figure still glowed with blue fire. This light was no more than a mixture of luminol and sodium hydroxide in water, with potassium ferrocyanide and hydrogen peroxide added. It was nothing but the cold glowing of a firefly.

Other chemicals had been released from the gross rolls of fat. They had severed the chains. And packed in the extra weight it had required to make up for King Udu, were many other chemicals.

The knife of the *Papa Loi* had begun to strike down at Pat Savage. The man of bronze was on the stone platform with a single leap. His hands waved. The *Papa Loi* shivered and fell on his face. The *Maman Loi* drooped forward. The old women went to sleep with their withered hands still in the boiling pot.

Masai warriors were no less than paralyzed. Some started to flee.

ONLY The Shimba realized the truth. Seizing a long spear, he drove it directly at Doc Savage's back.

There was something like the rumble of a human earthquake. The giant Renny unable to break his chains, had hurled his huge body upward. The heavy stake pulled from the ground. The big engineer was like a ball of hammering iron.

Though he could not use his fists, Renny beat The Shimba to one side. The Shimba snarled an oath in English. He crashed Renny's skull with the heavy haft of the spear.

The Masai warriors were rallying. They saw now this was something less than a manifestation of magic. The strange body that had been King Udu struck among them.

Spears were thrust straight at the man of bronze. Some of these he caught and snapped as if they were mere toothpicks. He whirled one huge Masai from his feet. Big as he was, Doc used the man as a club to beat his way to Renny's side.

"You're smart, but we'll get all of you!" rapped The Shimba.

He lifted a spear. Its point was at Renny's throat. Doc felt the wind of a thrown weapon. Another long spear grazed his head. It carried away tufts of the white hair that had seemed to be on the skull of King Udu.

The Shimba's blade plunged downward. It missed Renny's throat. The spear that had come close to Doc knocked The Shimba's thrust to one side. At this, the lion-clad man leaped toward the white man who had been hovering in the background.

His lion's head still concealed his features. Doc drove to interpret the Masai leader, but many of the natives had rallied. They were rolling in a wave upon the prisoners. Their oxhide shields protected them.

The man of bronze was forced by close fighting to permit The Shimba and the other white man to fade into the jungle shadows.

Renny staggered to his feet. The big engineer got to the stone platform. With his chain-bound body, he threw himself forward. He intended to shield Pat Savage to the last from the Masai spears.

Trapped by the spears, the man of bronze crushed several anæsthetic capsules. These halted a score of warriors. For a moment, they piled as an obstacle to Doc Savage.

But the charging line was wide. Hundreds of warriors were coming from the bush. Hope seemed scant for the survival of any of the prisoners.

Then came the rapid beating of several drums. The Masai halted. The wave of death receded. In the distance, toward the village, a new battle cry was arising. Gunfire suddenly outdrummed the tom-toms.

Ham's waspish body rattled his imprisoning chains.

"Doc!" he cried out. "They've executed a flank movement! The village of the Kokonese is burning!"

Thick, whitish smoke rolled upward in a cloud. Guns were exploding between the shrine of the Long Juju and the spreading fire.

Doc and his companions did not know this, but Monk, Johnny and Logo, with their new army of Kokonese, had been outflanked by a horde of Masai and other wild tribesmen. The rescue of old King Udu, as they still believed Doc to be, abruptly became less important to many of the Kokonese, than the saving of their homes and families.

Logo was unable to stay an avenging rush back to the village. The Kokonese, with modern rifles, returned to meet this new attack, to rescue their women and children.

In the meantime, Doc Savage quickly freed Señorita Moncarid and Ham.

Chapter XX

THE SHIMBA REVEALED

"SAFEGUARD Señorita Moncarid at all costs," instructed Doc. "With King Udu dead, she is the final hope of the Kokonese. None but she will ever rule under the Blood Idol."

The man of bronze was leading the others in a silent advance toward the village. Ham gazed in amazement at the dusky beauty of the young woman who had been Pat's companion.

"You mean Señorita Moncarid is of the Kokonese?" said Ham.

Pat Savage, a trifle white-faced, but quick to recover, gave Ham a superior smile.

"I have known that for some time," she said calmly. "With the king, her father dead, she is the last of the family line. She was taken prisoner by the Masai when a little girl. She is really the Princess Monca."

"We have no time to discuss that now," stated Doc. "Some of the Kokonese now are well armed, but the Masai and their allies are numbered by the thousands. No doubt The Shimba means to destroy the village, rout those who are loyal, then hunt us down."

Knowing now King Udu had been impersonated by Doc Savage, this had become the purpose of The Shimba. Many of his warriors had been sent to the attack on the village while the ceremony of the Long Juju was in progress.

Because of Pat Savage and Princess Monca, the man of bronze approached the village warily. Several times passing bands of Masai, this forced the small group to hide among the thick lianas.

At last they reached a rolling eminence. From this they could hear the battle cries and the screams of dying men.

The village was being deserted by a fleeing stream of women and children.

Kokonese were using the rifles to guard this line.

"Holy cow!" groaned Renny. "The king's palace is going up in smoke! Look! There's The Shimba himself!"

Once in the village, the thronging Masai were crowding around the flaming palace. The six, old counselors of the dead king sat on the ground and rocked their bodies.

Though many had fallen before Kokonese rifles, the Masai made up a seemingly unbeaten horde. The Shimba was directing a surrounding movement to capture these riflemen.

"Their ammunition won't last long against that mob," stated Ham. "Perhaps, Doc, we should retreat deeper into the jungle, while we have the chance."

"Remain hidden," directed Doc. "If you are discovered, employ the explosives!"

The man of bronze vanished as noiselessly as a shadow. He left with Ham and Renny several of the small globes, any one of which was sufficient to wipe out a hundred men.

As Doc disappeared, Renny suddenly let out a rumbling plaint.

"Now we're in for it! The Kokonese are out of bullets! They are falling back! We'll be caught in the massacre!"

A tide of retreating natives, with yelling spearmen driving it, came surging through the jungle.

"Now we are sunk!" rapped out Ham. "We can't use the grenades without blowing up our friends! We'll have to move!"

BEFORE they could act, the bush beside them parted. Logo, once of Long Island, appeared. In his tribal war garb, he was an impressive figure.

Renny would have swung a huge fist. Ham caught his arm.

Logo dropped on his knees before Princess Monca. From his belted Colobus fur, he produced a gleaming object. It shot out dazzling reflections.

"Princess Monca!" he exclaimed. "I have seen Doc Savage! Take the Blood Idol!"

Renny let out a whooping gasp. Ham stared in amazement.

"The Blood Idol?" said Ham. "Great Scott! It's a huge, red diamond! Was that in the teakwood box Doc received in Manhattan?"

Logo bowed his head. He smiled upon the dusky beauty who had been known as Señorita Moncarid.

"Fitting for Queen Monca," he stated quietly. "It is only part of the vast treasure of the red diamonds under the Kilimanjaro. I sent it to Doc Savage in New York for safekeeping. The leader of the Masai was seeking it there and brought about the assassination of Prince Zaban."

The explanation was hasty. Hoarse cries of Kokonese and Masai were coming nearer. Logo said, "Come with me quickly. We have one chance to escape. Perhaps Doc Savage will succeed in a daring stroke."

Princess Monca's garments had been torn from her arms. As the group pushed through the jungle, Ham saw the blue scorpion on the young woman's shoulder. The astute lawyer realized this was the mark of the royal family of Kokoland.

All around the little party, the bush crashed and echoed to the clash of warriors.

"Holy cow!" grunted Renny. "We'll never get out of this without blowing up some of your own people!"

"This way," said Logo, parting a green wall.

"Well, that is something to write home about!" exclaimed Ham.

One of the invading army's captured war tanks had been concealed. Before the Masai reached that spot, all were inside the steel fortress and Renny had the motor turning.

At this time, in the burning village, The Shimba's Masai warriors were emitting exultant yells. Others of their tribe were pursuing the retreating Kokonese.

One end of the king's palace was still untouched. The Shimba commanded some of the tribesmen to enter. They started carrying out some of the royal treasures. Stalwart Masai emerged, bringing with them the casket of Prince Zaban.

"Return it to the fire!" ordered The Shimba. "Let the body be destroyed!"

The order never was carried out. From one end of the village, roared two clanking Juggernauts of war. Before the startled Masai could decide upon their next movement, the tanks were upon them.

Some of the boldest stood their ground. The tanks' machine guns beat upon the air. The first bursts of bullets were directed over the heads of the tribesmen.

"Get into the bush!" yelled The Shimba. "We can wait!"

But his Masai were caught by the fever of fear. Those who were not already fleeing, were falling on their faces in abject terror. Among them were falling almost invisible glass objects. Terror was being replaced by sleep.

None, for the moment, heeded The Shimba. The smart leader apparently saw the uselessness of making a stand. He once more vanished from the scene of battle.

Doc Savage and Monk emerged from one of the war tanks. Johnny and two Kokonese tribesmen came from the other. Sleeping men lay around them. The old and wrinkled king's counselors were asleep with the others in the village street.

"I fear we are too late to save much of the palace," stated Doc. "But only a portion of the village will burn. Wait here. I will return to Pat and the others. They may still be trapped."

Monk let out a yelp.

"Look, Doc! There's another tank! Maybe them heathen grabbed it!"

MONK would have turned a machine gun upon the slowly moving tank as it approached, but Doc Savage interfered. The iron door of the tank slowly opened. First to emerge was Pat Savage. She gave one hasty glance at the burning palace and the sleeping Masai in the street.

"Some homecoming for the queen!" she exclaimed. "Monca, you haven't any throne left!"

"Queen Monca will have a much more modern throne," stated Logo, climbing from the tank with Renny and Ham. "A palace fit for a civilized queen."

Princess Monca stood there smiling.

"And fit also for the king," she said. "I would not care to rule Kokoland alone."

Logo, who had been William Smith of Long Island, rubbed his hands nervously.

"The words spoken in New York must of course be forgotten," he muttered.

"Well, I like that!" snapped Princess Monca. "Your proposal made in New York before you knew my identity is accepted! You can't jilt me now! If you do, I'll hide the Blood Idol and I'll—"

Doc Savage had glided close.

"Too many lives have paid for the Blood Idol to permit its purpose to be unfulfilled," stated the man of bronze. "King Udu sent it to Logo in New York, for safekeeping. Prince Zaban was murdered, though Logo's Kokonese tried to guard him. Some of the Masai were tricked to their death seeking the Blood Idol. I think Logo has earned his right to be called a king."

This was a long speech for Doc Savage. He might have explained more, but Pat Savage cried out.

"Count Cardoti! We thought the Masai had killed him! But he is alive!"

Doc Savage and his companions whipped around. With his clothing in rags, Count Cardoti came running from the jungle. His face was streaked with dried blood. He had every appearance of a man who had just escaped from the Masai.

"Doc Savage!" cried Count Cardoti. "You have beaten them off! I was staked in the bush! They intended to kill—"

The count quit speaking. A look of dazed surprise came over his face. Both hands clutched at something which suddenly protruded from his breast.

Count Cardoti fell forward, hands still clawing at the point of a spear. The weapon had come whistling from the jungle behind him. It had struck him squarely between the shoulders and pierced his heart.

Pat Savage covered her face. The man of bronze whipped toward the dead man, eyes searching the bush. Another man stepped forth. He was remarkably like the count in appearance. He spoke clearly.

I did that because he tried to double-cross me! He would have left me behind, and he would have told you I was the only one who played Shimba! He was my brother! When he was absent I took his place here! My brother had Prince Zaban assassinated!"

Doc Savage was moving swiftly. But the bronze man was not fast enough.

"As brothers of the blood, we plotted to steal King Udu's kingdom and brought the invaders!" cried the other Shimba. "Count Cardoti intended to replace King Udu! Now as brothers of the blood we die!"

The man cast himself forward. A short, stabbing spear in his hand was forced through his body. The Cardoti brothers, in whose vein had run the hot blood of the Spanish, or perhaps Portuguese, were dead.

A LITTLE later, Doc Savage said, "Yes, old Selan was working with Count Cardoti. I suspected Cardoti back in Manhattan. He was convinced I had the Blood Idol, so he decided to accompany us to Kokoland. That was why I returned the body of Prince Zaban."

"Then he would have killed Princess Monca," stated Ham.

"Count Cardoti did not suspect the identity of Señorita Moncarid until after we arrived in Africa," said the man of bronze. "But Logo knew. Yes, Logo had well earned his right to be king."

Pat Savage sighed deeply.

"And I miss my one chance of a lifetime to be a queen," she complained. "Count Cardoti asked me to marry him."